BENEATH THE SURFACE

TARA MARLOW

Wildlight
PUBLISHING

A NOTE FROM THE AUTHOR

CONTENT WARNING

This story contains content that might be troubling to some readers, including, but not limited to, death and/or dying, suicide, drug and alcohol use/abuse, abuse (physical, mental, emotional, verbal, sexual), and self-harm.

Please seek assistance if needed from the following resources:

U.K. - https://www.nationaldahelpline.org.uk or call 116 123 for Samaritans
U.S. - https://www.thehotline.org or 800 799 SAFE
Australia - https://www.respect.gov.au/services/ or call Lifeline on 13 11 14
EU Helplines - https://ec.europa.eu/justice/saynostopvaw/helpline.html

OR, call your national support line.

For Natalie. I am very proud to be your mother.

There are no secrets in life; just hidden truths that lie beneath the surface.

- Michael C. Hall

THE ROOM WAS dark and chilly, with only the moonlight for illumination. Grace woke, soaked in sweat, feeling lost and unsure of where she was. Images from the dream flashed through her mind. Blood-splattered walls. Loud, insistent sirens. Gurgling water. Sharp thorns from overgrown bushes. Stinging cuts on her arms. An abandoned trail. Someone yanking her arm, pulling her along. Running. Panting. Now, she was awake and short of breath. Her eyes darted around the room, trying to remember where she was. She placed her hand to her pounding chest. The room smelled damp, like wet towels marinating on the floor for days. Relief overwhelmed her. She was in her bedroom. She took a deep breath, but the images lingered.

Another nightmare. Just another nightmare. That was all. Eventually the fear, and a feeling she couldn't quite place, subsided. The song from *Frozen* popped into her head. Oh, for fuck's sake. She hadn't heard that song in years. How did she still know every word, even now at seventeen? Still, it was enough to break her from the night-mare's hold. She picked up her damp hair, the curls clinging around her fingers, and splayed it out behind her on the pillow. Minutes ticked by. She stared at the ceiling as sleep eluded her. The *Frozen* song continued. *Let it go, let it go.*

She leaned over the side of her bed and grabbed her phone from the floor.

It read: 1:43 a.m. She groaned, placing the phone under her pillow. She still needed to get through the rest of the night.

The apartment was quiet. Too quiet. Her father had yet to come home. Maybe he was dead, she mused. Wouldn't that make things easier? Knowing she wouldn't have to face him tonight, she pulled the worn covers up around her. She hugged her knees against her chest, trying to fit comfortably on the tiny bed. At five feet ten inches, it was a challenge. Sighing, she flipped over, doubled her deflated pillow in two, and began crafting her favourite dream: her own bedroom with lots of fat pillows and thick, warm bedcovers blanketing the enormous bed. Bedside tables, stacked with books, and simple lamps to read by.

Shivering at the bitter cold coming through the cracked window, she added long, heavy curtains to her wish list. Ones thick enough to keep out the winter cold. Geez, she would be happy with windows she could actually open, snapping her back to reality. Hell, she was lucky to have a roof over her head. That hadn't always been the case.

She returned to her nightmare. Images of red flashed through her mind. She rubbed her hands along her arms, reassuring herself there were no cuts. But she felt as if there were. Everything in the dream felt real. The nightmares were always the same and they were coming more frequently of late. What was that about? She didn't understand it. She yawned, pushed the thoughts aside, and turned toward the cold cinderblock wall. Thinking again of the image of the beautiful bedroom she would one day have, she finally drifted back to sleep.

Grace's crusty eyes flew open, when she heard her father's keys thunk against the front door. When they hit the ground, he cursed loudly, his hand slamming against the door. She scoffed, knowing it was probably to balance himself. Grace eased up from her pillows, and reached for her phone underneath. The brightness seared her eyes, sending pain zinging into the back of her head. She adjusted quickly. The display read: 2:36 a.m.

Shit.

"Grace! Get tha fuck… here!" His words slurred more than usual. She could barely understand him. "Now!"

The front door slammed behind him with a metallic thud. She was sure the neighbours next door were aware of her father's return. Who was she kidding? The whole complex probably heard him. How could they not? Especially at this time of night.

She eased out of bed, her heart in her throat. Trouble was coming. Taking the risk, she reluctantly opened her bedroom door a little. The light blinded her momentarily. She smelled her father before she saw him, a stark aroma she couldn't quite place.

"Yes?" she whispered.

"I said, git tha fuck ou here!" he bellowed. Neighbours definitely heard that one. She opened her door a little further, her eyes adjusting to the brightness, assessing the scene. There was no way she was going to walk out to him, so she kept the door as a barrier between them.

Her father slouched at the front door, his stained jeans hanging off his hips, his hands thrust into his pockets. He was tall at six feet, but his thinness made him look gaunt in his oversized blue t-shirt. His greasy brown hair flopped onto his forehead, accentuating the deep lines etched into his face. He looked a decade older than his fifty years. His boots were wet even though it was not raining outside. She hated to think from what. She opened the door further but stayed where she was.

"Dad, I have school tomorrow," she said, leaning heavily against the door. She was exhausted, but her mind was on high alert. She could feel his anger from across the room.

"Dun give a fuck wha' ya doin' tomorrow. I's what ya did t'day. Stealin' fr'm me now?" God, he was plastered.

"What? No." She bolted upright, defensive against the accusation. Stealing? What the hell did that mean? "I mean, I grabbed some money from your wallet. We needed food, and you were still asleep this morning when I left."

"You stup'd bitch. I need'd tha money."

"Sorry, but we had nothing to eat," Grace mumbled, picking at her cuticles.

"Wha? Ya job does'n pay now?" She wanted to scoff. He knew it didn't pay much, but at least it covered the rent he never seemed to have the money for.

"It's not enough to live on," she said. He had to know that.

"Don't backtalk me!" he roared, his speech now clear.

Before she knew it, he was across the room and dragging her back toward him by her hair. She yelped, trying to twist and find her footing at the same time. She could smell the cheap beer and that unfamiliar stink. Damn, he was using, but she just didn't recognise what.

"I'm sorry, Dad," she cried. "I wasn't stealing, I swear." He pushed her hard against the wall. The force knocked the wind out of her.

"Ya don know wha you did." His sticky fingers dug into her arm. She locked eyes with him. He blinked and for a moment, she saw him, her father, looking at her with a gentleness she hadn't seen in a long time. He released his tight grip a little. He seemed confused, as if in a daze. Was this fit over? He blinked again, and her father was gone. All that was left was rage, dilated pupils and the rank smell that was making her feel nauseous. Not knowing what he was on frightened her more than his fists. At least his fists were somewhat predictable.

"It was only twenty dollars," she gasped when his grip retightened around her arms. She knew what was coming.

He whipped her around and pushed her up against the wall, pinning her arm behind her. Her face was wedged flat against the cold brick. She whimpered in pain, too afraid to scream. She didn't dare move, knowing she was in a position where he could snap her arm. He'd done it before.

"You're a fuckin' thief." His rancid breath expelled against her cheek. She felt the spittle left behind as he hurled the accusing words at her. "I don' need this shit. One more time an' you're out, ya hear me?" She nodded, tears in her eyes. To be certain she was listening, he lifted her arm higher up her back, driving unbearable pain. His left fist rammed into her kidneys, leaving her breathless. He released her, and she crumpled to the floor. He kicked her squarely in the ribs, then stumbled off to the bathroom.

"Stupid, fuckin' bitch."

She lay on the floor until she heard the bathroom door close. Then, leveraging herself up using the nearby chair, she limped quietly back to her room and softly closed the door. Ignoring the pain, she rushed to the chair in the room's corner, tossed her uniform to the floor, and shoved the chair under the door handle. She needed to protect herself from another beating tonight.

She listened for her father's movements. The splash of urine in the bowl carried in the small apartment, and ignoring the flusher, she heard the bathroom tap rush with water. Grace stayed at the door, hunched over in pain, listening, waiting. She could barely move, barely breathe. Everything hurt. But it wasn't her first rodeo. She knew with his kick that he'd broken a rib. Maybe two.

Grace held her breath when she heard her father stumble past her room. She jumped when he beat his fist against her door. But he kept going. He slammed his own bedroom door with another expletive. She yelped. Then, finally, the place was silent. She released her breath, knowing he'd be passed out, splayed across his bed, still dressed in his soiled clothes. What the hell was going on with him?

Guessing his rage was doused for the night, Grace took a deep breath but felt the pain shoot through her like she'd been prodded by a hot poker. She'd be sore for weeks. She needed to avoid him. Usually, he left her alone for a week or two after the beatings. But lately, something had changed. It left her feeling uncertain. No, not uncertain, scared. Only months before, he was predictable. Now she didn't know what to think. She was anxious. Her nails were surrounded by strips of bloodied raw flesh and wisps of dangling skin, her cuticles eager to be picked.

Grace tiptoed to her bed, reached down, and doubled her two thin pillows over to sleep in a more upright position. It was a trick she learned last time. She eased herself down on to the bed and froze when the springs creaked. Thankfully, the only sound coming from her father's room was his snoring. She lay her head against the pillows and let her breathing return to normal, at least as normal as it could be with a broken rib, then let the tears stream silently down her face.

Four more months. Just four more months. Turn eighteen. Finish high school. Freedom. That was her mantra. She couldn't wait to move on from this miserable life. She was exhausted, emotionally and physically. Getting beaten up was no dream. She missed her dad. She missed the fun times they had in the past. But that was a long time ago. Since moving to Sydney, things had changed. She didn't know why and and there was no way she was going to ask him. She just had to get out.

But then what? Dread filled her. She had no money to live on, no way to support herself. She covered the rent of their cheap, mouldy, bottom level apartment in North Ryde, but she could barely afford to buy groceries with what was left. She was stuck. And yet, she had no choice but to get away from her father. The question was how? Her friend Lowell offered his place to stay, but… No. he didn't need her mooching off him. She would work something out. She had to. Whatever her father was into now, he was becoming dangerous.

Maybe she should stay with Lowell, even if it was for a little while. At least until she found somewhere else. But….no. His apartment was tiny, barely enough for him. And, he'd just opened his own business. He didn't have room for her, and he certainly didn't need some seventeen-year-old to deal with either. Still, Sydney was expensive. Maybe she'd have to get out of the city, find somewhere cheaper. But where?

Four more months. Just four more months. Turn eighteen. Finish high school. Freedom.

Yeah, she didn't need this shit either.

2

THE NEXT MORNING, Grace rose slowly from the bed. Her entire body screamed. She pulled the covers up in a half effort to make her bed, then reached down to pick up her school uniform from the floor, almost passing out from the pain. It would take her longer to get ready this morning. She listened for noise in the apartment, and only heard guttural snores from her father's room. She moved cautiously to the chair, dislodging it from under the door handle. Her hand slipped. The chair, striking the door-knob, sounded like a gunshot ricocheting off the walls. Grace froze. She listened for movement. Nothing changed.

She opened the door slowly and padded softly to the bathroom. Closing the door, she wished for a big, sturdy lock. She looked in the cracked mirror, glued at a slant against the wall. Her face reflected the pain she was in. Her bloodshot eyes, normally a moss green, were darkly shad-owed underneath and swollen from crying. She poked her fingers at the puffy mounds, wishing they would magically deflate. Giving up, she slowly bent and gently washed her face. She reached for her towel then groaned when she realised she'd left it in her room. She looked around and considered using her father's towel laying in a pile on the floor, but she couldn't remember the last time it had been washed. Instead, she wiped her face with the sleeve of her ragged t-shirt.

Looking back into the mirror, she raised her fingers to put her long, wavy chestnut-coloured hair into a ponytail, but pain sliced through her midsection like a sharp knife passing through her. She left her hair down, but placed a few strands in front to cover the scar from a past infraction. When brushing her teeth, every movement, every brush stroke brought tears to her eyes. Grace desperately wanted to lie down and let the pain take over, but she had to get through it.

He hadn't always been this way, she reflected. Her mind flashed to when they'd been bush camping a few years earlier. She'd been fourteen, maybe fifteen. She cherished those days of sobriety. Her father ran out of beer after a few days, but he didn't pack them up to leave like he usually did. At first, he was jittery, but soon began joking with her. She hadn't seen him like this for ages. He spent days teaching her about native bushes and how they thrived, surprising her with his knowledge. When she asked how he knew so much, he admitted he once owned a landscaping business, then promised her pots full of flowers once they got to Sydney. It never happened. Instead, this non-human being she lived with now had taken over her father. Drugs had won. Life with him seemed a lot different now.

She spat toothpaste into the sink and rinsed her mouth. Lifting the top of her worn out t-shirt, she inspected her midsection. Shades of crimson and purple spread across her ribs. She quietly opened the cabinet drawer under the sink and reached into the very bottom, grabbing the elastic bandage she kept there. A hospital visit for treatment was out of the question. The first time she tried that, the staff saw right through her lie and called Child Services. When they arrived home, her father whipped her with a belt, then told her to pack up. They moved again. New location, new name. Her name was Grace Robinson then. She had no clue what her last name really was. They'd been changing names with every move since she was five. She didn't know why. She'd asked, of course. *Something happened years ago,* her father told her. *Better to be safe than sorry,* he said. Whatever that meant. Since then, it was all she could do to remember their latest last name. Not knowing why pissed her off. Didn't she have a right to know why they were constantly moving? Hell, even to know who they were running from? At first, she didn't know any different, but changing schools, losing friends, learning on her own when she wasn't in school, it just made her angry. She once told him she didn't want to move constantly. That earned her a backhand. She was resigned to it now. Better to go along with it. That's why she created her mantra, her plan. She would get out of this crazy life. Four more months.

Brushing the memories off, she lowered her top back down and headed back to her room. She rummaged to the bottom of her backpack to find the ibuprofen she kept there. It would help with the inflammation and hopefully, her raging headache. She popped a few tablets into her mouth and swallowed them dry.

Within twenty minutes, dressed in her school uniform, backpack hanging precariously over her shoulder, she locked the front door behind her. When she got to the front of the building, the bus stop only metres away, a car dared to drive in the bus lane to beat peak hour traffic. But her bus was right on its bumper, laying on its horn, forcing the car back into the traffic.

Shit, she was later than she thought. She ran to flag the bus down, ignoring the fire in her mid-section. Halfway there, the tip of her black boot caught on a crack in the footpath, sending her sprawling. Her knee slammed into the pavement. She screamed in pain, then looked up. Shit. Shit. Shit. She saw the contents of her backpack splayed around her. She whipped her head around to the front door behind her. She couldn't let her father see what was in her backpack. Relieved to find the doorframe empty, she looked back and quickly retrieved the only things she cared about. The silver bracelet her mother gave her when she was born. A heart, a flower and a book charm, all dangling from it. A birthday card, with Snoopy smiling boldly on the cover, given to her by her mother for her fifth birthday, the last birthday she remembered with her. And a hand stitched bookmark, a tortoise and a hare, her favourite movie when she was young, from her grand-mother. She carried these things with her always. They were sacred. She called them her 'absolutes'. She didn't care about anything else they left behind. But these things? They were forbidden. They were things from the past. Things she was supposed to have gotten rid of years ago.

But they were hers. Treasures. Connections. So, she'd hidden them. And she knew if her father ever found them, found out she kept them… She shook her head. She didn't want to consider that.

In front of her, the bus squealing brakes signalled its arrival. Ignoring the pain, Grace gathered everything up as fast as she could and, remembering the reason for the beating the night before, ran her hand down to the bottom of her backpack. The five hundred dollars she stashed in a hidden pocket was still in its place. She'd never tell her father about that money. It wasn't a lot, but it was her escape money, in case she needed to get out fast. And things were looking more and more like that time was approaching.

3

LATER THAT AFTERNOON, Grace sat at her usual table in the Daisy Café at Macquarie Centre, located just down the street from her apartment. At this time of day, the café was busy with local university students, as well as professionals from the surrounding business parks. The only thing that differentiated the students from the professionals were the heels and polished shoes. The students didn't care; the professionals did, but they still ordered the same drinks.

Come five o'clock, the centre would be packed with families. When Grace was new to Sydney, she was shocked to see Macquarie Centre always bustling, no matter when she visited. But late-night shopping on Thursdays brought in the families in droves. Not surprising. The place was a major shopping hub for the north west and north shore areas.

Now, almost every table in the café was taken, many with books splayed across tables or shopping bags at people's feet. And almost all had winter coats thrown over the back of their chair. There was a line of people waiting to order, and an equal number waiting on their orders, all with their heads down, their eyes glued to their iPhones.

Grace looked around. For three days in a row, she felt like someone was watching her. She hated the feeling, but it was one she'd lived with for years. Being on the run, she was always looking over her shoulder. But now, it felt different, more like stalking, and she didn't like it.

Movement caught her eye. Shit. A tanned guy, with dirty blonde hair and keen brown eyes approached her table. Maybe he'd been the one watching her? Dismissing him, she returned to her books and focused on her English assignment.

"Hey," Keen Guy said.

Silently, Grace groaned. The guy stood at the edge of her table, and out of the corner of her eye, saw his ripped blue jeans, sparkling new Converse and a coffee in his left hand, his right one shoved into the pocket of his jeans.

She looked up and smiled briefly, noticing his university hoodie before returning to her papers. He was good looking in a grungy way, but he gave her the vibe that he knew he was. Sorry, dude. Not interested. Grace kept her ear buds firmly in, happy she'd found the cheap pair in a local thrift shop.

"What are you working on there?" He persisted, ignoring her dismissal. He slurped his coffee, looking down at her expectantly. When she didn't respond, he snapped his fingers in front of her. Great. He was *that* kind of guy. She pulled one earbud slowly from her ear and looked up at him, one eyebrow cocked.

"What are you working on?" he asked and stuck his snapping fingers back into his jeans pocket and slurped again.

"Homework. Which I need to finish." She moved to return the ear bud, but she wasn't fast enough. He reached down and leaned on the chair across from her.

"Homework? Like, a uni assignment? What's your degree?" God, she hated the dumb ones. They took extra effort. She held his eyes with hers.

"No. I'm writing an essay for my high school English class," she said, emphasising the words high school. She should have left her school uniform on. That usually deterred the fray, but she started work in an hour.

"Ah, sure. Well. Good luck with that," he said, his hand releasing the chair quickly as if scorched, before he scuttled away. Yep. See ya. She replaced the earbud. Tell them you're still in high school and they run for the hills. Besides, these guys had a university campus full of young women across the road, ripe for the picking.

Despite the guys constantly hitting on her, she was thankful for the café. Normally, being on the ground floor of the centre, tucked into a corner, the café was quiet. She couldn't study at home, especially when she didn't know if her dad would be there, and it was definitely better than the library. The local library was a joke. Between the noisy young kids sitting through tutoring lessons and screaming toddlers, it was enough to do her head in. Plus, the cafe was convenient since she worked part-time upstairs. She could easily deal with the unwanted attention, and considered wearing her school uniform to help with that, but she only owned one. The coffee spills she constantly inflicted upon herself were problematic, and her work outfit was way easier to clean than her school uniform.

By the time Keen Guy left the café, Grace was lost again in her creative writing assignment. She was working on her major assessment for her Extended English class. The teacher gave them the freedom to write in whatever format they wished. It was one reason she'd chosen the elective. Grace decided on a comparative piece about women's rights between first and third world countries. Her dream was to be a human rights journalist, so this was a task she was eager to delve into. It was certainly a stretch from her classmates' topics. One of her classmates chose to write a fictional romance, another a comparative piece between football players and fanaticism. Her teacher expressed astonishment at Grace's topic because it was far more complex than most of her classmates' choices. When the teacher asked why, Grace explained it was because of a book she read, written by a young Pakistani woman who had overcome seemingly insurmountable challenges. It inspired Grace to set a goal for herself. And to set her mantra.

A short time later, the chair across from her was pulled out. She snapped her head up, expecting to see another young hopeful taking a seat. Instead, her friend Lowell placed his bag down.

"Easy Jelly." Lowell grinned down at her. "I'm not the predator you were expecting."

"Thank God for that," she said, removing her earbuds. She smiled openly at her English friend. Her cheeks flaming red despite herself. She still got embarrassed when he called her Jelly. "Just fought another one off."

"It's what you get for being so gorgeous, love." Lowell said, standing behind the same chair Keen Guy had been leaning against moments earlier.

"Ha. Gorgeous in my stained work shirt, wrinkled black pants that are desperate for a wash, and dirty hair?" Lowell chuckled at her joke, although it was close to the truth. It reminded her to buy shampoo. And do her laundry soon.

"I didn't think you were working today?" Lowell said, flipping his messenger bag open to fish out his phone.

"Yeah, I am. Since my boss loves me, she called me in. She said she's happy to throw me any spare shifts," she said, glancing down at the time on her phone. "I have twenty minutes before I have to go."

"Good thing you work upstairs! You won't be late," he teased. She was notorious for being late with him. "I'm grabbing some tea. Need a coffee?" She opened her mouth to answer, but Lowell quickly held up his hand.

"Wait. How much have you had today?" he asked, his right eyebrow raised.

"Only four. I'm okay for now. Thanks though," she said, giving him a sassy smile, knowing he hated her coffee habit.

"Geezus, Jelly. You need to cut down. Four at your age is about three too many." She smiled. She loved Lowell. He was like a protective older brother. She shrugged and quickly winced, the pain reminding her she couldn't do that today. She tried to hide it from Lowell, but he caught her distress.

"Jelly?"

"I'm okay. Go, get your tea." He looked at her worryingly, shook his head, then walked to the counter to order. He looked very… what was the word he liked to use? Dashing. That was it. Yes, he looked dashing today in his dark grey dress pants, paired with a pressed white shirt under a black button-down vest. She watched him greet the barista. The woman beamed her radiant smile in return. Everyone who met Lowell loved him.

They'd met eight months earlier. Lowell had come into the Daisy Café for the same reason she did, the quiet. On the day they met, Lowell literally caught her at the same counter where he currently stood. She'd passed out at the café's pickup counter. She was mortified, but she hadn't eaten in days and admitted she had gone all 'jelly-legged' right before. From that day on, the nickname and their friendship stuck.

After that, they began to share a table, especially during busy times. Lowell was initially working on a business plan for the yoga studio he'd just opened. At the time, he was working three jobs just to save enough to rent a space and buy equipment. Three jobs! She could barely keep up with her part-time one. But he was the most determined person she'd ever met. Not that she'd met that many. Now that the studio was up and running, he was refocused on his business degree.

They caught weird looks from other people, once they started hanging out together. She could understand why. She was a lanky and uncoordinated seventeen-year-old high school student, with her hair usually in a very untidy top knot, always carrying a worn out thrift store backpack. In contrast, Lowell was a good looking, very well put together, twenty-three-year-old black man from England, who always carried an expensive leather messenger bag. They knew they made an odd pair but they didn't care what other people thought. They were close friends now, with more in common than any observer would believe.

Her father's words rushed into her head: *Blend in. Don't bring attention to yourself.* Hanging out with Lowell was the opposite of that. But her father suspected nothing of her friendship with Lowell. She made sure of that.

"So, what's going on with you?" asked Lowell, when he returned with a ladened tray holding a white teapot, a cup in its saucer, and two muffins sitting precariously on matching white plates. He unloaded his tray and pushed the blueberry muffin toward Grace. He knew it was her favourite, and she had finally given up asking him to stop buying them for her. She was grateful. She'd eaten only a banana and a piece of toast over the last two days, but she would not admit that to Lowell. There were some things she needed to keep to herself.

"John up to his usual tricks?" he asked. He waited for her answer before diving into his messenger bag. Grace tried to avoid his gaze, but he knew the signs from personal experience.

"Jelly, are you okay? Did your father use you as a punching bag again?"

"Wasn't bad. I'm fine," she answered and picked up the fork to take a bite of the muffin. "Thanks for the muffin."

"Hmm," he said, frowning. "I worry, you know."

"Yep, I know. Seriously, I'm okay. It wasn't too bad this time. Nothing that I haven't dealt with before. But come on, tell me how your class was this afternoon?" she asked. She loved hearing his stories, and she needed to change the subject. Lowell worried, but she didn't want to talk about it. She was sick of talking about it, thinking about it. She would rather live vicariously through someone who'd faced the same music and was now dancing to his own tune.

"Jelly. This… whatever is going on with John, it's becoming more frequent. And you're good at hiding it, but this is me."

"I'm okay, Lowell. I wouldn't lie to you," she said, taking a bite of the muffin, crumbs falling into her lap.

"Yes, you would. About this, I know you would," he said, and she grimaced.

"Want to know how I know?" he asked. She nodded, reluctantly.

"Your cuticles are torn to shreds. Ravaged. You pick at them when you're anxious and, I daresay, when you're scared." She looked down at her nails and then shoved them under her legs to hide them. "Why do you stay with him, Grace? I don't get it. I mean, he's your father. But…?"

"I can handle it. He wasn't always this way. I was thinking this morning about the garden he promised me. Maybe I'll suggest a few plants for our balcony. That might bring him around." Lowell shook his head, but Grace felt in her heart that her dad wasn't a lost cause.

"You know that's probably not the case, Grace. I mean, last week he had your head in the toilet. This week, well, it looks like you're barely moving."

"He isn't as bad as you make it. He taught me how to play the guitar, remember? And he asks about school, reminds me how important it is…" although she didn't want to admit it had been at least six months since he'd asked.

"Those are all traits of control, Grace. He wants you to know how to play the guitar, so you can support yourself in a pinch. And the grades? He's probably making sure you leave home. It's about ego and control. I know what it's like Grace. My father is the master of it."

"I know you worry, and I've promised you, I'll call you if it gets bad or if I need an out. For now, I have a plan and I'm focused on that. Turn eighteen…"

"… Finish high school. Freedom. Yes, I know your plan. You've told me many times. Seriously, Jelly, move in with me. If you don't want to do it now, at least plan on it when you turn eighteen. Just be vigilant, Jelly. Seriously. I don't think it's as safe as you think." He leaned over to the chair next to him and pulled his laptop from his bag, placing it on the table.

"I promise I'll be careful. Now, tell me about your class?" she pushed. Lowell's eyes were cast with doubt. She smiled. Lowell shook his head, then took a sip of his milky tea, a gesture that always settled him. Finally, he took the hint.

"It was good, but you'll be sorry you missed it. We've been rockin' with the oldies this week," he said, smiling, then picked up his fork to take a bite of his own muffin.

"Has Annie been up to her old tricks again?" asked Grace, drinking the last of her lukewarm coffee, thinking of one of Lowell's favourite clients. She loved the Annie stories. It was like listening to a funny children's book. Annie stood just under five feet. Her hair was bright pink, and she always wore bold red lipstick. She was like the crazy grandmother everyone wanted. Grace certainly did. Most of Lowell's clientele were senior citizens. He was smart to advertise at the nearby independent living centre, to get his studio going. Grace loved to tease him that these women, some in their eighties, only joined to gawk at Lowell. When Grace joined one of his classes, Annie shared that Lowell was a hot commodity at their centre, being the sexy young yoga teacher from England with the delicious accent. He drew quite the crowd.

"No, Annie's fine. She's what makes the class fun. She brought in a feather boa today and you'd think she was reliving her twenties. Or she secretly wants to be a stripper. I'm not sure which. Oh, speaking of feather boas, I have that book I was telling you about." He reached in and pulled a paperback from his bag. "This, Jelly, was a fabulous read. The main character? Incredible." She thanked him for it and tucked the book into her backpack.

"Anyway," he continued, "I'm really sorry I haven't been around all week. Been crazy with classes, and I've finally unpacked my boxes at home. God, I'm so glad I moved. The place is minuscule, but it's mine. I'm so happy to be out of the clubhouse. Being the only gay man in a house full of rugby boys, it's not as exciting as you'd imagine. I'm glad to be rid of the locker room smell!"

He placed his fork on the edge of the plate and watched her close her books. She needed to get to work.

"Here," Lowell said, wrapping the rest of his muffin in his paper serviette. "I know you've had your head down and you probably haven't eaten anything solid in days. Take the rest of my muffin. You look skinnier than the last time I saw you."

She felt heat flush her cheeks. Some days she hated that Lowell knew so much about her home life. She knew he was concerned. He also knew what living in an abusive house was like. His worry came from a genuine place.

"Don't worry about me. I'll pick up a bag of salad to eat on my break," she said and took a huge bite of the blueberry muffin he bought her. With her mouth full, she added, "And this muffin will be enough until then."

"Grace, seriously? You need more than a bag of salad and the occasional muffin. And this stuff going on with John? You seriously need to consider moving in with me. I'll make room for you."

"Lowell, please, not today. I get things suck for me right now, but I'm fine. I can handle it." But was that true?

He reached over and squeezed her hand. She laughed, swatting his hand away. She glimpsed his semi-colon tattoo on his hand near his thumb and remembered what he'd been through himself. Now, he was finding his own way. He had his yoga business, and he was finally living on his own. She would not interfere with that.

"Right. Work," she said, and devoured the rest of the muffin in two bites. He thrust his own muffin toward her. Knowing he wouldn't give in, she took the muffin and stashed it in the side pocket. She rose slowly from the chair, ignoring the grave look on Lowell's face. With fast plans to meet on the weekend, she threw him a kiss and left for work.

Dodging shoppers, she headed toward the escalators, and thought of Lowell's offer. She would have loved to crash at his place, but she wouldn't be able to live with herself if it slowed him down. There was barely room for one. It was stupid to even consider it. She owed it to Lowell not to stand in his way, no matter what the cost. He was finally on the path he'd dreamed of. She wouldn't impede that.

Coming off the escalator, she weaved her way toward the supermarket where she worked. Suddenly, the reality of her life came crashing back when a screaming toddler ran out from a nearby shop, tripping her. Stumbling forward, the marble floor closed in, her knee slamming down on the hard surface. Pain shot through to her ribs. She screamed wildly.The child's mother dashed out, glaring at Grace with scathing judgement, as if Grace was the guilty party in the incident. Bitch.

Slowly picking herself back up, Grace realised whatever was going on with her father, things were getting serious. Lowell's question reverberated in her mind: Why stay?

4

A WEEK LATER, Grace was back at her usual table in the café. She was glad work was over. It had been a crazy Saturday morning in the supermarket, mainly with manic mothers picking up organic nut-free snacks and oranges for their kid's netball or football teams. Some mums were chatty at her register, but others just screamed at their bickering kids. Now, her head was pounding, and she needed more caffeine.

She was meeting Lowell at three. Now, barely past two, the café was quiet but for the sound of the barista manically grinding beans, getting ready for the afternoon onslaught. The aroma of the espresso made her swoon. God, she wanted another cup, but told herself to wait until she finished her assignment. She couldn't afford to be indulgent.

Grace looked over to the opposite side of the café. There, a guy stared at her, chewing on his pen. His stare was making her uncomfortable. But wait, no. He wasn't staring at her. He was thinking, deep in concentration. She'd noticed him before. Like her, he came in to work. And, like her, he kept to himself. Sometimes, he worked on his laptop. Today, he was scribbling in his notebook.

She guessed the guy was about twenty-four, twenty-five at most. He'd been in line behind her a few weeks before and had almost knocked him over when she turned around. She hadn't seen him and spilled her coffee down the front of her work shirt, right before her shift started. The stain had been a bitch to get out.

But that day, she'd noticed every detail about the guy. How his light brown hair was flecked with blonde from the sun, cut short, but still long enough to make him look roguish. How his cornflower blue eyes were rimmed by long, thick eyelashes that curled just at the end. And his laugh lines, how they were etched deeply into his cheeks, making his skin look baby soft. She felt the blush blossom on her cheeks, thinking of their collision. Most times she bumped into someone, they told her to 'watch out'. But not this guy. He was kind enough to ask the barista for a towel.

Grace snapped out of the moment when his attention returned to his notebook, and he returned to writing, now furiously. She placed her hand on her burning cheeks, then set back to her own task.

Ten minutes later, a shaking hand placed a mug by her side, coffee spilling over the rim. She looked up. Standing before her was The Guy. He smiled at her, placed a note beside the cup, and walked away. That was weird. She opened the note.

Hi. My name is Daniel. I swear I'm not stalking you. You

seemed so intent on your studies that I thought you'd appreciate the caffeine. The barista says it's your usual. Enjoy.

Grace watched Daniel leave the café. At the exit, he looked back at her, smiled, then he was gone. Huh.

An hour later, she followed Lowell to his car. They were heading to his new apartment. He was excited to show it to her without all the packing boxes. The shopping centre was a madhouse. It was hard enough on a normal day to walk side by side, but today it was impossible. Kids chased one another through the crowds, their parents yelling after them. Mothers with strollers demanded space, hitting the heels of the unsuspecting when they didn't comply. Older couples sauntered, holding up the hurried mass behind them, causing havoc whenever they stopped to admire shop windows. With the cold weather, it brought in more people than usual. No one wanted to be outside today. But Saturday afternoons were always like this at Macquarie Centre.

"You know, I noticed this guy in the café today," Grace finally said, once they stepped on the escalator to rooftop parking.

"Oh, my God, Jelly. You actually noticed a… guy?" Lowell put his hand on his chest in mock shock.

"Oh, shut up. Yes. I noticed him. Most of them are Uni jerks, just looking to hook up. But this guy, I don't know. He comes in, orders a coffee, then puts his head down to work. He usually stays about an hour. But today, he bought me a coffee. He said nothing to me, but he left a note." She said it in a boasting tone, happy she'd scored a free coffee.

"Great. That's all you need. Someone else to feed your coffee habit!" Grace noticed Lowell was careful not to use the word addiction. The last time he'd let that slip, she went ballistic on him. It wasn't like her coffee was laced with alcohol or that it was as serious as drugs. Snapping to, she realised Lowell was still talking.

"… he didn't speak to you? Has to be something wrong with him."

"Don't be mean. Maybe he's shy? Maybe he respected I was studying and didn't want to bother me. Doesn't matter anyway, he's too old for me."

"Like, thirties?"

"No! More like twenty-three, twenty-four? Around your age I guess. He looks like a uni student. I don't know."

"Maybe he's what they consider a mature age student? Like me. Besides, you aren't jailbait anymore," he said, when they reached the parking level.

"The guy looks… well, I don't know." She couldn't say hot, even though she'd instantly thought that when he'd left the note. She'd rebuffed so many other guys before and didn't know why this one was different. Maybe it was because he didn't try to hit on her. Plus, he was pretty cute…

"Come on, Jelly. Try to describe him. I am sure I would have noticed him before. And I can't remember any guy sitting at the café I haven't pointed out to you already." Reaching the door to the parking garage, Lowell opened the door for Grace, then held it for a woman and her three children as they shuffled through, the mother mumbling her thanks. Lowell pointed toward his car.

"I don't know… he's there at odd hours. And after school, like me. He's tall, taller than me. His hair is kind of light brownish-blonde, cut short, and, um, he has these really vivid blue eyes." She looked sheepishly at Lowell, who arched an eyebrow at her.

"He looks like he works out, I guess. He wears jeans a lot with boots. And long sleeve dress shirts. Oh! Wait! He was wearing a suit a couple of weeks ago." Lowell groaned. She knew Lowell liked guys in suits, especially pinstriped. Lowell said nothing but unlocked his car with the ancient remote.

"And he has laugh lines, right here in his cheeks…" she said, sighing, and slid into the passenger side.

"Seriously?" Lowell said, slamming his door. "And you snagged him into buying you a coffee? I'm surprised a guy got past your usual rebuff. Hell, I'm shocked we're even talking about a guy. Talking about hot guys is usually my thing."

"He is kind of hot," she whispered, finally admitting it out loud. "And I haven't snagged him. He just bought me a coffee. It was, I don't know, sweet. His name is Daniel." Lowell turned the key in the ignition, and she reached for her seatbelt.

"There's nothing sweet about it, Jelly. Especially if he's older. Be careful. And a guy who looks like that? He has an agenda. He's definitely looking to hook up." She doubted that, but he was cute. How bad would it be if she went out with him? She shook the idea from her head. No. Her life was complicated enough without throwing a guy into the mix.

"Well, he can want all he likes. I'm not an idiot. He won't get far; I can promise you that. And let's be honest, if he is interested, he'll be just like the rest of the guys. If he's as old as I think he is, once he finds out I'm seventeen, he'll run for the hills."

"Just be careful. I mean, I think you should date, but if he's older, that may be more than you're ready for. Just don't say I didn't warn you. And a guy with moves as smooth as that? He sounds slick. You need to be on the lookout for what's next. Just keep in mind that if a guy is buying you a coffee, what does he want in return?"

5

LOWELL DROPPED Grace at the intersection near her apartment around seven that evening. Driving her directly to her front door was too much of a risk. *Blend in,* words her father often repeated, popped into her mind again. Her friendship with Lowell was one she kept secret, so she always insisted on being dropped at the corner. There would be hell to pay if her father ever found out about Lowell.

Waving goodbye, she was amused by his concern for her safety. If only he knew about some of the situations she'd been in before. Like the time an old guy started groping her in a brothel, while she waited for her father. The old guy couldn't keep his appointment after her retaliating kick to his groin. Or the time her father got mixed up in a bad drug deal and she had a knife pulled on her. She'd sweet-talked her way out of that, saving both her and her dad. Walking home at this time of night was like heading to the library on a Saturday morning. People were everywhere. She could fend off an attacker if she needed to. Just not her father. He was different.

Walking up the cracked concrete footpath, she thought of Lowell's plans for the night. He was heading out on a date with a swimmer he'd met at the local pool. She chuckled, thinking of his harried pace as he got ready. He was so nervous about what to wear, but eventually settled on jeans, a button-down shirt, and one of his much-loved vests. She loved that he was giddy. But who could blame him? He was getting on with his life. It had been a rough start for him. Being in the closet wouldn't have been easy. But now, out of his father's dictatorial clutches, the life he dreamed of was just beginning for him. The new guy sounded hot, but Lowell was also extremely talented in describing a guy's physical attributes, sometimes in too fine a detail. She only hoped he didn't fall in love too quickly this time. The last guy devastated him, dumping him a month after they'd met.

But then, what did she know about dating?

She climbed the grungy stairs at the entrance of her apartment block, thinking of the possibility. Yeah, she'd plenty of interest, from both guys and girls. Some even asked her out, but they were probably foolish dares, especially from the guys. Dating was definitely not part of her plan. Nope. She had a goal.

Fishing her keys out of her backpack's side pocket, she thought of Daniel. Hmm. She would consider a date with him. He was very... what word had Lowell used to describe his date? Fi...Fine. That was it. Would she describe Daniel as fine? No, not really. He was too rugged for that, then thought about what Lowell had said earlier.

Something about Daniel having an ulterior motive. Maybe she'd risk it. She thought of Daniel's blue eyes and his soft laugh lines. Yeah, those things could suck you in.

At the front door, she shifted into stealth mode, listening for any sign her dad was home.

"Please don't be home. Please don't be home," she said in an inaudible whisper. She listened intently. Quiet, thank God.

She put the key into the rusty keyhole. She opened the door to the dark apartment and hit the light switch. The empty beer bottles sitting on the table made her heart pound. Still, she heard no sound. Her eyes scoured the small apartment, but she held the door open. She was ready to run if she had to. She turned her head to see into her father's bedroom. The bed looked like it hadn't been made in a month, and his stained clothes from the night before lay in a heap. Otherwise, the room was empty. The bathroom door was also open, and she heard nothing coming from the kitchen. She released her breath and gently closed the front door, hearing the quiet click behind her.

Her mind raced. Her father had been home at some point during the day for this many bottles to be laying about. Hints of her father's mood were hard to find. She picked up the empty Tooheys beer bottles from the white Formica table. Traces of white powder lay on the surface. She felt her heart drop, and her hands shook. Shit. Beer and ... something that looked like cocaine. That was not a good sign.

Panic filled her. She thought of calling Lowell to ask if

she could stay the night. No. No, she couldn't do that to him, especially when she knew how much he was looking forward to his date. Maybe her dad wouldn't be back? Sometimes he'd be gone for days. Maybe this would be one of those times. Hope clouded her judgement. She thought to Lowell again and realised she had a shift the next morning. Even if she could stay, Lowell's place was too far to make it for her seven o'clock start. Sure, she could take the train, but she'd be relying on a connection, and she read maintenance was scheduled for that train lines over the weekend. Plus, the buses were on limited runs at that time of the morning. Crap. She would just have to risk staying.

Grace grabbed the kitchen cloth, rinsed it under cool water, and then looked at the coke on the chipped table. She laughed grimly, thinking some cokehead would still get a buzz from what remained. She wiped it away. She didn't care. She didn't want it anywhere near her. She knew what it did to people, the destruction it caused. And if it was her dad's coke? Maybe this would teach him a lesson for leaving traces behind. Ha. Who was she kidding? He wouldn't even remember it was there.

She burned a few matches to get rid of the rank smell from the stale beer, dreaming of how nice it would be to have a vanilla scented candle. Just a simple scent, she mused, something to take away the dank smell of the place. But they cost money she didn't have. She ran water through the soiled cloth. Someday she would fill a room with lots of scented candles. She was sick of the smell in this apartment. It was burned into her nostrils. But whatever this crap was, the smell that overlayed the mouldy dank? She hated that more. She was sick of dealing with her dad's bullshit.

She walked back to her bedroom, then stopped, looked around. It was so different from Lowell's space. His place was inviting, theirs stark. Her bedroom was basic, cold, and she could see mildew growing out of the crack along the ceiling. Lowell's apartment was on a quiet, tree-lined street and it felt peaceful as soon as you drove on to the street. Grace could hear honking from impatient drivers rushing home from work, even with their apartment in the back half of the building. She hated this place. Sick of the discarded food wrappers that found their way into the hallway, blown in from the street. Tired of sidestepping vomit on the footpath from drunk University students. Tired of tripping on the cracked step going down to the laundry. She was even over the dirty washing machines in the communal laundry, breaking down as soon as they were fixed. She was ready to move, but as she looked around, she knew she was lucky to have a dry place to sleep. Hell, lucky to have a space that was hers. That hadn't always been the case with them moving around.

She tossed her backpack on to the single bed, pushed up against the wall lengthways. She took off her jacket and threw it onto the wobbly brown wooden chair, now sitting in the corner. Beside it was the scratched-up dresser, left behind and graffitied by the previous tenant, which held her entire wardrobe: two pair of pants, a pair of jeans, a pair of shorts that were way too small for her now, a handful of t-shirts she'd found at the op shop, and her work uniform. She considered herself lucky to even have the drawers. Her clothes and books were normally stuffed into her stained duffel, the one she'd found abandoned on the side of the road.

She looked at the walls and shuddered. The walls in Lowell's new apartment were painted a soft grey with large, framed prints hanging on them. Her walls were off-white and stained from God knows what. And that ever present mildew that seemed to grow every day. She avoided the walls at all costs. Lowell's space was fresh smelling, like clean laundry. Grace had scrubbed their place so many times, but no matter what she did, the dank smell remained. Her apartment was at the other end of the spectrum from Lowell's. She learned not to move her dresser. She'd tried a few weeks after moving in, and a mass of tiny cockroaches came scurrying out. There was no bedside table. No wardrobe to hang anything and there were no blinds. It looked like they moved in with only their bags. Which was close to the truth. They moved in with one box that held a stained set of sheets for each bed, two thin worn towels, their sleeping bags from camping, and some basic kitchen supplies. The rest she'd picked up from op shops and council pick up days. She knew they were lucky to find a place so cheap, so she couldn't complain too much. It was better than living out of her dad's rusty, ten-year-old car. It stank worse than the apartment.

Grace walked to the cracked, grimy window that over-looked the narrow backyard. It was a stretch to call the concreted area a backyard, but that's what it was for many. Two kids kicked a ball amongst clotheslines set against the rickety wooden fence-line. A line of washing lay limp for days in the constant shade. The sight depressed her. The kids playing in this environment made the scene look even more dismal. This place was transitional, just as she and her father were. Living in places like this was a drawback to moving around a lot. *Being on the run*, corrected the voice in her head.

Brushing off the thought, Grace plucked her school uniform from the back of the chair and shook out the wrinkles. Mrs. Goodfellow, her form teacher, berated her the week before about her lack of ironing. Goodfellow. What an ironic name. The woman was the school uniform police. Sure, her uniform was never pristine, but she'd apologised to the witch. She wanted to tell the woman she didn't own something so frivolous as an iron. But why bother? She'd probably get detention for talking back. The teacher was old-school with no heart. She probably lived in a house with a cosy wood stove, polished floorboards and a vegetable garden in her sumptuously large, grass-filled backyard. She probably owned not only an iron but also an ironing board!

Yeah, an ironed uniform wasn't at the top of her priority list. Food was, and there was little of that as it was. Her pay cheque working part-time at Woolies never quite covered what they needed. When she'd taken the twenty dollars from her dad's wallet the week before, she'd just paid their rent to the real estate agent. She had no money left, and she needed to eat. Did her dad even make money anymore? God knew what he lived on, besides beer and, well, whatever, flashing to the white powder that had been on the table. A jar of store-brand peanut butter was the only thing left to eat in the apartment, and it was nearly empty.

Normally, she existed on coffee, toast, and peanut butter, and had for years. When Woolies started offering free fruit to children, an incentive for better eating and occupying kids while their parents shopped, Grace felt like someone had given her a million dollars. Now she was older, it was harder to snatch up a piece of free fruit on her way out.

Grabbing leggings and a t-shirt, sniffing it to make sure it was clean, Grace headed to the bathroom. It was easier to shower at night. With her dad out most nights, she relished the privacy.

She flinched when the water hit her bruised midsection. Turning, she let the hot water cascade over her shoulders for a moment, letting the water ease the ache a little. She reached up for the shampoo on the windowsill, wincing at the pain as she washed her hair, then gave up on conditioner when the effort proved too painful. When she finally stepped out of the shower, she felt the cold air hit her steaming body. Grace quickly redressed her ribs with the same stinky bandage she'd used that morning, eased on her clean clothes, and headed back to her bedroom.

Remembering the white powder on the table, she moved her jacket to the top of her dresser, grabbed the chair, and wedged it under the door handle. While she didn't believe it would stop her father in a howling rage, she hoped it would deter him. Or, more realistically, slow him down so she could prepare for the inevitable. She'd tried moving the bed against the door one time. But the noise it made, when she needed to get out in the morning, made it impossible. Then there was the cockroach infestation if she moved the dresser. She hated that the chair was her only real protection.

Grace settled into her squeaky bed and read through the first three chapters of the book Lowell loaned to her. It was an engaging story so far. What did they call women like this back in the day? Her English teacher, Miss O'Donnell, used a word last week that made her laugh. Gumption. That was it. Yes, women with gumption. It was definitely something Grace didn't have, she mused.

Around nine, she heard the front door open. She tensed, but she didn't hear the door slam. Weird. That wasn't normal. She held her breath, waiting for sounds of movement. Her fingers dug into her cuticles.

"Grace?" She heard her father's keys hit the table and something else that sounded like plastic. Then the smell hit her. Chinese food. "Grace? I have food. Come get some."

There's my dad. But, remembering the scene on the table earlier, she was still a little wary of leaving her room.

"Come on, it's getting cold." Her stomach rumbled. Lowell fed her sushi around five, but she was still hungry. And the aroma was intoxicating. She'd ordered Chinese takeaway only twice before with her dad. Both times her dad had been sober, but the beer bottles and coke from before didn't show sobriety to her. Her stomach rumbled again. She risked it. She shed the lightweight bedcovers and quietly lifted the chair away from the door.

"There you are. Wasn't sure if you'd gone to bed." Her dad looked sober, contrary to the evidence from the table, and he looked like he'd taken a shower too. "Grab a plate. I grabbed extra egg rolls. I know you like those."

She did. They were her favourite. She sometimes

bought two in the food court because they were cheap. She looked at her father with astonishment. On the table sat eight containers, all open and all full. Steam lifted from them. One was filled with beef, another chicken. Noodles lay piled in two. Egg rolls were in another. Her mouth watered, watching her father pile food on a plate.

"Where'd you get all this food?" Suddenly, she felt like she was ten again. Had he found a job somewhere or… no, she couldn't think of that. That had been a horrible time. He'd robbed a petrol station when she was twelve, while she sat in the car with the engine running. They'd eaten like royalty for a week. They'd even found a place to live a few weeks later. But then the money ran out. She knew that whatever this was, it was short term, and he'd want to move again soon.

"Ah, got it from a place I was doing a job for. They had a slow night."

"What kind of job?" she asked, the question slipping out before she realised she really didn't want to know.

"Just a kitchen job. Temporary." A job was a good sign. Maybe it would lead to another? Maybe they wouldn't be moving after all? Her father sat at the table and started eating the fried rice mounded high on his plate.

"How's school?" he asked. "Keeping your grades up?" Her dad had been strict about that once. He called her the smart one when he was sober. Then, when high, he called her an idiot. She didn't know what was going on now, but she appreciated his sobriety for the moment. That was a good thing, but she still wondered whose coke it was.

"School is going okay. Grades are still good." He pointed to her plate, encouraging her to eat. She picked up her fork, wary, but her stomach reacted to the food before her.

They bantered about what subjects she was studying, and she told him about her English assignment as they ate. She wasn't too hopeful, but it was nice to see her dad being himself again.

Her father told her about another job lined up the following week and gave her fifty dollars to buy groceries. The gesture shocked her. What happened to last week's rage over twenty dollars? She took the money and slipped it under the rim of her plate. He continued talking, sharing a story about the restaurant owner. His eyes were clear. His voice soft. This was so different from the week before.

"I was thinking about the garden we talked about," she said, hesitantly. "You know, when we were in the bush those few weeks. With the tent. We have a patio now. We could put some plants out there." She knew she was taking a chance, but that time was one of the better ones over the years.

"Well, let's see if I can find something more permanent before we do that," he said. She thought about suggesting a job in landscaping, since he mentioned his business years before, but her father was up, washing his plate before she could get the question out.

"I'm going to head out again for a bit. Put whatever's left in the fridge when you're done. It'll be nice to have some food in the fridge again, won't it?" He smiled down at her. She bit into her third egg roll and plastered a goofy smile on her face. He laughed, kissed her head, picked up his keys, and headed back out the door.

Yes. There was her father.

6

SHE SENSED it before she even saw it coming. The slap came down across her cheek, hard and fast. She gasped, shocked at the intense burn, then recoiled against something thorny. She reached around and felt warm blood where the thorn pierced her tiny fingers.

"RUN, I said!" Her father's face was suddenly in hers. His breath was horrendous. A musty, rotten smell with a hint of something she couldn't place. He looked crazy mad. His eyes were bulging, his pupils the size of pinpricks and surrounding them, red, spindly lines. The vein in his neck pulsed visibly.

Something jammed into her back. This felt different. It wasn't the thorns she felt before. She looked behind her to see blood covering a red suitcase. A lot of blood. With that moment of hesitation, her father's hand, red and scratched, reached down and yanked her up by her arm.

"MOVE!" he hissed, and pushed her forward. She stumbled. It was pitch black, and she had no clue where she was, but she could hear voices nearby. She wanted to scream for help, but her

father scared her witless with stories of little girls that cried for help. Not wanting that to happen to her, she picked herself up and started running.

"FINALLY!" her father said in a rasped whisper. He was on her heels now, dodging branches as they ran.

The dream fast forwarded. It was the same scene, but now she was ten years old, about five years later. She did not know where they were running to. But the house they had been in, the house with the red suitcase by the front door, was no longer home. Nor was the house after that. Or the house after that. Grace looked back. A woman stood by the door of their original house. She held her hand out, saying something Grace couldn't hear. Grace wanted to run back to her, but her father was dragging her by the elbow in the opposite direction. Red filled the dream. Red everywhere.

Grace woke, gasping for air. She was sweaty, but ice cold. When she finally opened her eyes, the overhead light blinded her. Shivering, she got up and hit the switch. Just as the bedroom went dark, she heard the front door open. Grace stood dead still. The door slammed shut with a resounding thud. Experience told her not to alert her father to the fact she was up. As if working on instinct, she moved to the corner of her room to grab the chair. Then, tiptoeing back, she wedged the chair under the door handle.

She heard her father swear, then felt the entire apartment vibrate when something crashed against a wall. Shit. So much for the sobriety.

"Where's my fucking beer!" her father screamed. His

pounding steps shook the entire apartment. He approached her door, but she put her body against it, hoping with her added weight, the barricade would hold. The door handle turned, and while the door held, she knew she was no match for her father in a rage.

"What the fuck?" He tried again. She pushed all her weight again against the door. "Open the fucking door!"

"No," she responded, knowing she was taking a risk.

"Then where the fuck did you put my beer?" he yelled, slamming his hand against the door. She jumped, but stayed where she was, leaned in more.

"You've drunk them all. Look inside the recycling. The empty bottles were on the table when I got home."

"Open the fucking door!"

"No. Go look in the bin. The empties are there."

"You drank my beer?" He slammed his body against the door. Grace pictured the door breaking against the chair, but it only wobbled. "Open the fucking door!"

"NO! You drank them before you left." She dared not mention the white powder she'd found.

There was silence. Then a grunt. She heard him walk away, open a cabinet door, slam it shut. Then the fridge opened, and she heard a clink. Oh, thank God. A bottle was left. Good. Maybe that would sate him for a while?

"Leave my fucking beers alone next time!" he hollered. She kept still against the door, unsure of what more was to come. She heard the groan of the futon in the lounge room.

Still, Grace leaned against the door for what seemed like forever. She was too scared to move. She dug into her cuticles once more, grimacing when she struck a nerve in her nail bed. Soon, loud snoring reverberated through the apartment. She took a steadying breath, then walked as gingerly as she could to her bed. The sheets were still damp from the nightmare. She was so ready for this actual nightmare to be over.

Grace stretched out, her feet sticking out over the end of the bed. Her heart was still hammering, but now, the familiar dose of disappointment overwhelmed her. She knew her dad was still inside that crazed person. She had to believe that. Why else would he bring home Chinese food and give her money for food? He hadn't always been a drunk or an addict. Maybe…. But hope lost out to tears. She was stupid to think he was clean, if the white powder was anything to go by. Why had she hoped for anything different? She'd heard the same empty promises before. It was like being on a merry-go-round. Why did she think one moment would change things?

Her thoughts shifted to her dream. Why did she keep having the same nightmare? Always running. Running had been much of her life, so she wasn't surprised by that aspect. But why was there always so much blood? She shivered. The one thing that really confused her, the thing that bothered her the most, was the red suitcase by the door. That was new. It appeared in her nightmare three times now. What did the suitcase mean?

7

Grace was up half the night, waiting for her dad's rage to resurface, but exhaustion finally took over. She startled awake when sunlight hit her eyes. She panicked, grabbing her phone from the floor to check the time. It was dead. Remembering she left her charger at Lowell's, she flew into auto mode.

Forty-five minutes later, Grace ran into the school compound, composed of two-story red brick buildings clustered around a large concrete courtyard. It was just her luck that first period was at the very back of the school. Getting caught being late wasn't quite at the top of her list. Rules dictated she required a late note from the school office, but explaining why was too risky.

Hitching her backpack higher on her shoulder, Grace found her English class. She already had a major target on her back being the new girl. Being late didn't help. Standing outside the classroom, waiting for the right moment to enter, she looked like a wreck. Her uniform was a mass of wrinkles, and she was relieved most of it was covered by her stained school jumper. She'd forgotten to wash that, too. She looked down at her scuffed boots and hoped she didn't run into Mrs. Goodfellow. She didn't just look like a wreck; she felt like one too.

Grace peered through the door. Her English teacher faced the whiteboard. Great. She could sneak in without notice. One of the popular girls, Sarah, sat in Grace's usual seat. Sarah, with her crisply ironed uniform and her shiny blonde hair pulled high into a ponytail, tied off by an equally crisp blue ribbon. Crap. She scanned the room and found an empty seat right in the middle of the classroom.

She opened the door quietly and made her way to the vacant seat. Before Grace could reach the chair, Sarah noticed her.

"Did you forget about school today, Grace? Too busy whoring yourself out to remember?" The words caught Grace mid-stride. Sarah was a vicious one, but she suspected it was because Sarah's boyfriend had asked Grace out first and Sarah despised being second choice in anything.

"What..." Grace, breathless, flushed scarlet, frozen behind the vacant chair. The teacher turned toward her, her back straight, her eyes sharp as daggers.

"Grace. Nice of you to join us this morning. Please, take a seat and start working on the essay on the whiteboard." Miss O'Donnell, her 2-unit English teacher, stared cooly at her before turning to Sarah. "And Miss Williams? Please refrain from making such vulgar comments." The teacher walked to her desk and sat primly in her chair.

Grace slunk into hers and watched Miss O'Donnell's

hazel eyes survey the room. Taking the nudge, Grace opened her workbook and begin the Shakespeare essay. Sarah snickered and muttered something nasty under her breath. Grace ignored her. Moments later, Miss O'Donnell rose from her seat and glided toward Grace. Saying nothing, she simply handed Grace a note, then walked to the storage room at the back of the classroom. Not sure what else to do, Grace read the note.

I allow one 'under the radar' late pass per year for each student. This is twice. See me after class. By the way, the debate sign-up is today. I expect your name on it.

Grace fumed while re-reading the note and felt herself unravel. She was emotionally raw with little sleep. She couldn't do more than she already did. The forced expectation from O'Donnell was the last straw.

At the end of the class period, Grace walked to the front of the room where the teacher sat, uneasy yet determined. Grace shook, the tears in her eyes contradicting the anger she felt. The note became a crumbled ball in Grace's white fist.

"Miss, I'm sorry I'm late. I know it doesn't look like it, but I'm doing my best to be here and to be on time. I just…" Grace sighed. She sagged visibly; her shoulders hunched. She was exhausted trying to blend in, exhausted keeping up with her studies, exhausted just trying to live. Grace gathered her strength and straightened, looking Miss O'Donnell in the eyes.

"While I would love to join the debate," she continued, "I don't have time. Between working on assignments, preparing for the exams, working a part-time job, and dealing with... some emotional stuff at home, I just can't take on one more thing. Please believe me when I say this, Miss O'Donnell, I am working very hard so that I can leave, what I consider my version of hell, as soon as I possibly can." Her knees weakened, she hoped they wouldn't give out on her. She knew she shouldn't be speaking back to the teacher, but she just couldn't take it anymore.

Miss O'Donnell sat in her chair, her mouth agape. Grace didn't know why. Plenty of kids talked back. Maybe it was because Grace never had before. Composing herself, Miss O'Donnell stood, straightened her perfectly ironed, periwinkle blue top over her crisp black trousers and looked right at Grace.

"Well Grace, thank you for your honesty. I do believe you'd have a strong voice for the debate. Your essays offer a solid argument. I thought this would be an opportunity to give your voice that power as well. But I appreciate your time constraints." Grace, thinking the berating was over, turned to walk out the door and stumbled over the chair behind her. Miss O'Donnell grabbed her arm to stop her from falling. Grace gasped, sucking in a wheezing breath.

"What's wrong? Are you okay?" the teacher asked. Grace faltered.

"I'm fine," she said through gritted teeth. "Anything else?" The teacher looked at her for a long moment and finally shook her head.

• • •

At the last bell, Grace stuffed her books into her backpack and followed the crowd out the door. At least school was done for the day. She still had a four-hour shift tonight.

"Grace? May I see you a moment please?" Miss O'Donnell called out from the teacher's lounge, just as she was heading to the school gate. Shit. What did she want now? Grace looked to the ground, trying to recall what time her shift started that night. Was it six o'clock, or five? God, she wished her phone was charged. Six. It was the normal time, but there'd been some switching with the roster lately. She thought that was right. Work was the place she couldn't afford to be tardy. She needed the pay cheque. Needed the job. She looked up at her teacher and nodded tentatively. Miss O'Donnell ushered her into the over-crowded staff room, where Grace took a seat next to the teacher's desk. Some of her recent assignments were spread out.

Great. First the note this morning and now… this? Whatever this was. She couldn't afford to fail Year Twelve either.

"So," the teacher began, settling into her seat. "What are your plans after high school, Grace?"

"I…" Grace hesitated and then decided it best to be up front about her goal. "I want to be a human rights journalist."

Miss O'Donnell smiled. "Specific. Great. That's an ambitious goal." She sat back in her chair.

"I believe, with some fine tuning, you could excel in your exams and be on your way to that life. From what I can see, you're dedicated." The teacher placed her hands over the splayed-out papers. "You're smart, and the chosen subject for your English major work assignment is in line with your goal." Grace's eyes widened, staring at the teacher with skepticism. How the hell did she know about her major work assignment? She wasn't her teacher for that subject. Hmm. She didn't trust this turnaround after this morning's wrath.

"Your Extended English teacher shared your major work with me," the teacher continued. "I think you'll do well. Have you done any research on it yet?"

Grace felt obligated to share what she discovered already, and Miss O'Donnell shared additional insights with her. Surprisingly, Grace found the information helpful and would research further.

"Don't be afraid to go for the dream, Grace. I know first-hand how complex this world can be... and how accepting it can be, if you give it a chance." Grace stared at her in disbelief. She didn't understand the turnabout, considering her teacher had not shown this much interest before. It made her wary.

Miss O'Donnell leaned forward and told Grace that since their meeting that morning, she'd received feedback from the rest of Grace's teachers. This made things even more weird. Grace looked at her with suspicion.

"Your maths, while solid, could use some extra attention. Mr. Martin has given me some additional work for you, areas, he said, you are weaker in. He also said, if you have questions, see him directly. In fact, all your teachers told me that. We all believe you to be a strong student."

"Thank you," mumbled Grace, unsure of what else to say. Something wasn't right. The teacher seemed to pick up on her hesitation and sighed.

"You gave me some insight into your home life, Grace. You have a part-time job, fine, but the emotional stuff you mentioned, that worries me. And, earlier, when you cried out when I tried to catch your fall? Well, that concerns me more. You don't look well, more tired than I'd expect a normal kid to look like. I need to know if you are okay." Grace's back went up. When teachers zeroed in on her, that usually resulted in an impromptu move.

"Yes. Fine. Just a few rough nights at home," she said, trying to throw off any concern. The last thing she needed was Child Services snooping around, especially with her father's erratic moods. And, she really didn't want to run again. She just wanted to finish out the year at this school and then she'd be free.

"Do you have help? Support?" Miss O'Donnell probed. Grace hesitated, then decided to give the teacher what she wanted to hear, she nodded. Yes, she had support from Lowell.

"Okay, I'll have to trust you on that for now, but I'm here if you need me, Grace. I have my suspicions of what's going on at home," she said. Grace sat up a little straighter. The teacher put her hand out and covered hers. "Don't worry. You're past the age of my legal obligation to call Child Services. But Grace? I'm here for you. Whatever is going on, I want to help in any way I can."

Miss O'Donnell looked Grace straight in the eye. "I am here for you. For anything. I mean that." She handed Grace a piece of paper and, reading it, was shocked to see the teacher's name and mobile number. Why? Seconds passed. Grace knew she should say something. Something to placate her anyway.

"Thanks. But I'm okay. Really." Grace bent her head to avoid eye contact. What was going on? How many other students had Miss O'Donnell given her number to? She stowed the piece of paper into her backpack.

"Okay, switching gears a bit. Have you looked into scholarships for university?" the teacher asked. "That may be an avenue for you. You mentioned a part-time job. The government also has programs providing financial help. You can apply for the Youth Allowance Student Payment with Centrelink."

"I have looked, yes." And she had, on Lowell's suggestion, but learned that funding was not available to her. She would have to give them detailed information she didn't have.

"Well, I have some ideas and some contacts, so leave that with me. Here's another question I'm curious about, and then I'll let you go, I promise. I have seen what the kids are like here, heard the things they say to you, but I never see you defend yourself. Why?"

Grace knew the answer but wasn't sure how it had anything to do with her grades. Besides, why would the teacher even care?

"Why bother? They are going to believe what they want to, anyway. I'm new. An easy target. No matter what I say, no one will hear it. All I can do is keep my head down and keep looking toward the goal. I won't be here much longer, so why bother stirring the pot?"

Miss O'Donnell looked at her with sympathy. Grace waited for her to spout the bullshit she'd heard from teachers about bullying. It never made a difference. Kids could be cruel. Just as adults could be. Surprising Grace, the teacher said nothing, then stood. Grace followed her to the door. While still cautious, the teacher's concern touched her.

"Sorry to have kept you, Grace, but I hope it was worth your time. I do want you to know I am on your side. Contact me, anytime. I am here to help."

Grace left at five, even more determined to get the year over with, all with her grades intact, and her plan solidly in place. Knowing that the teacher couldn't legally call Child Services was a nugget she would cling to. But if her father knew the teacher had spoken to her and, God forbid, learned she'd handed over her personal information to help her, they would be on the run before morning.

Suddenly, she saw her future at risk. It may not be Miss O'Donnell calling authorities, but now she was on the radar of the other teachers. It wouldn't be easy, but she had to call Lowell. Things had changed with her father. She realised that now. And today, she could see her future clearly. It was finally within reach. The last thing she needed was her father's instability to mess that up.

8

Grace saw Daniel walk into the café. She hadn't seen him in a few days. Not since he'd bought her a coffee. He glanced over and smiled, then continued to a table on the opposite side of the room. Today, he wore a pair of lived-in jeans, a faded chambray, long-sleeve shirt rolled up to his elbows, and boots that looked to have their own story to tell.

"Focus Grace," she mumbled. A guy, no matter how cute he was, would not distract her. She had to get this assignment ready to turn in, so she put her head down and got back to work.

"Hi. Sorry to interrupt. I'm getting a coffee. Would you like one?" Daniel asked. His cornflower-blue eyes were more vibrant than she'd realised. He stood a comfortable distance from her, unlike the other guys who came to hit on her. Lowell's words rang in her ear: *Be careful, Jelly. He's probably just looking to hook up.* She stuffed her hands under the table and began picking at her cuticles.

"Oh! Thanks, but no. And um, I got your note. I'm not interested in going out," she stammered.

"Who said anything about going out?" he replied, smiling. She could see the laugh lines clearly now. The flutter of a thousand butterflies took off inside her stomach.

"Well, most guys..."

"Ha! I just figured you'd like a coffee. Every time I'm in here, you have one in front of you. Nothing more."

Hmm. He looked younger than she thought. Maybe closer to twenty. Most likely a university student. Just like the others.

"What are you studying?" he asked, looking down at her notebook. There it was. Bye-bye, cute boy. She continued picking at the broken skin around her fingernails.

"The H.S.C.," she answered, waiting for him to run in the opposite direction.

"Seriously?" Seeing the shock on his face nearly made her laugh out loud, but then his face turned into a broad grin. That wasn't the reaction she expected, nor was it the norm.

"Yes, I'm in Year Twelve." Grace fiddled with her hair, unconsciously moving a strand across the scar on her forehead.

"Cool. What's your name?" Cool? Really? She hesitated.

"Grace." He smiled. Ugh. She felt weird things inside her stomach.

"So Grace, what's your plan for next year? University? A gap year?" he asked. Words escaped her for a moment. No guy had asked her that before. Not even Lowell.

"Uni. Studying journalism," she said, then hesitated to add more. Saying it out loud, especially twice in one week, made it feel like an outrageous dream. She moved her hands back to her lap.

"Impressive. Most finishing Year Twelve don't know what they want to do. So, why are you studying here and not at home like most kids doing their Higher School Certificate?"

"I guess I'm not like most kids," she responded, throwing a sassy tone at him. Geez. What possessed her to say that?

He smiled and her face burned scarlet when she met his eyes again. She was drawn to him, but it was more than that. She felt hot when their eyes stayed locked.

"Well, I'll let you get on with it. Are you sure that's a no on the coffee?" he asked, breaking the stare. She nodded and Daniel left her to order, but not before tossing a look back at her, one corner of his mouth lifted in a smile. Lowell's words rang once more: *Be careful.*

She spent the next hour with her head down, sneaking glances at Daniel, catching him looking at her too. She felt something, a buzz, coming from him as well. He seemed interested. Why else would he buy her coffee? Her emotional radar was going haywire.

When she finally went home, Grace settled in with a book. Her legs dangled over the edge of the futon, her head resting on her bunched up towel. Her assignment was done, and she didn't expect her dad home for hours. But at the sound of a key in the door, Grace sprang upright. She jumped off the futon, grabbed the towel, and was halfway to her room when her father bellowed her name. She turned around and was surprised to see a woman with him.

John stood at the door with his arm slumped around the woman's shoulders. She had greasy blonde hair and a teal green shirt, stained and tight around her ample breasts, her skirt barely covering... anything, really. Her fingers, tipped with long acrylic pink nails, held a cigarette, smoked almost to the butt. She teetered on scuffed white stilettos that were at least two decades old.

"What are you doing here? Aren't you supposed to be working?" Her father spat. His face flashed with anger before turning to disgust.

"I'm not working tonight. I... I was just," she spluttered, then bolted to her room, closing the door behind her. She leaned against it, her heart racing. A woman? Here? With her dad? Her father had never brought a woman home before. Grace lay down on her bed and opened her book, but it was difficult to focus on the text. After trying for twenty minutes, she leaned down beside the bed to return the book to her backpack. Oh shit. Her backpack. It still lay on the dining room table. And her 'absolutes' were inside it. What if the skank went nosing around? She needed to get her backpack, and fast.

In a cold sweat, she pressed her ear to the door, but heard nothing. They must have gone to her father's room. She swallowed a wave of disgust, imagining the woman... no. Slamming her eyes tight, she tried not to see it. Now she couldn't unsee it. Focus, Grace, she chided herself. She had to get her backpack. It was her... everything. She cracked open the door and peered out. Her backpack was dangling off the edge of the dining table. She pulled the door wider and stopped when it creaked. She squeezed through the opening and was almost at the table when a strange squeal, like a pig at the trough, caught her attention. Her father's pants were around his ankles and his long, bony fingers dug into the woman's hips as he fucked her from behind. His eyes were closed, and he held a pained look on his face. The woman was bent over with her skirt hitched up, her pink tipped fingers caressing her own nipple. The woman looked over and delivered a death stare. Grace shuddered involuntarily.

The scene immobilised her. She didn't know if she should laugh or scream, but she was too afraid to move. Too afraid that even her breathing would alert her father to her presence. But she couldn't just stand there either. A crooked smile rose from the woman's mouth, and she jiggled her hips slightly. Her father opened his eyes. Shit. The woman winked at her.

"Get the fuck out of here, you stupid bitch!" Grace's father roared, seeing her for the first time.

Grace grabbed her backpack and ran back to her room.

She sat on her bed, trembling. Scrubbing her face with her hands, she tried to erase the image from her mind. The woman was pure evil. Maybe they would leave? She should have left, she realised with a silent groan. Gone to Lowell's place, not back to her room. Shit. Could she sneak past? No. She was trapped now.

"Please, please, leave me alone," she whispered. She tried to calm herself, rocking back and forth, taking deep breaths. When that didn't work, she opened her book again, but the words were fuzzy. She dug into her backpack and felt the money nestled in the secret pocket at the bottom. She may need the money sooner than later, but would it be enough?

She dove into the side pocket to retrieve her phone when the front door slammed shut. Flinging the bag aside, she bolted up to move the chair against the door handle. But it was too late. Her father was there, flinging her door open.

"What the fuck was that?!" he demanded, blocking the entire doorframe. Grace looked at him, arming herself with the chair in front of her. Her eyes, wide.

"I'm s-s-sorry, Dad. I... I needed my school bag." He grunted, then picked up the backpack from her bed. He looked undecided as to what to do with it. Her heart was in her throat. Grace knew there would be serious repercussions if he found the hidden cash. Rather than looking inside it, he threw it hard against the opposite wall, spilling the contents. She dared not look down at the mess and hoped he wouldn't either.

"Why are you here? And why don't I get any fucking privacy?"

"I'm sorry. I didn't mean..."

"No. No, you never mean nothing," he said in a mocking tone, like a schoolyard taunt. He took a quick step toward her and grabbed the chair, throwing it to the side. The force of his backhand across her cheek flung her backwards. Her shoulder slammed against the chest of drawers, the corner drawing blood.

"Just leave me the hell alone. I never asked for a kid. Next time I have company, I don't want you here. Got that? I don't care where the fuck you go, but this is my house. Do you hear me? Mine."

"Yes," she whispered meekly. She stood in front of the dresser with her hands raised in front of her, silently begging him to stop. He grabbed her shoulders and shoved her backwards into the drawers. The force knocked the wind out of her. She dropped like a sack to the floor. Grace remained lying there until she heard the front door slam once more. The relief was palatable, but the episode soon overwhelmed her. When would it stop? The physical pain was fleeting. But this feeling of hopelessness, the uncertainty of what his rage might inflict, that anguish was too much. Blinding tears flooded her eyes. She lay there for what seemed like hours.

When the pain eased a little, she surveyed her room. Books and trinkets were scattered everywhere. She rolled to her knees and slowly picked up her treasures. When everything was back in its place, she crawled into bed.

Yes, she heard her father loud and clear. In reality, the place was more hers than his, since she paid the rent more often than he did. But the lease was in his name. Or someone's name. The name he had stolen.

She knew she wasn't safe anymore. Things had changed too much. She would move in with Lowell, even if it was for a few weeks. This nightmare couldn't continue. Lowell encouraged her many times to move in with him. He warned her it would get worse as it had with his own father. And still she clung to the fact that her father was not all bad. Maybe she was wrong? Other than the Chinese dinner recently, she hadn't seen the father she missed in a long, long time. She began a text Lowell, but hesitated over the keypad. No. She couldn't. She couldn't do that to him. There had to be another way.

But maybe, just maybe, her life depended on her moving in with him after all. She remembered that feeling of freedom and hope when she left the school grounds. Yeah, it was time.

9

THE RESULTS of last night's trauma left her body aching. She'd woken with blood on her sheets and purple bruising around the gouge in her shoulder. Now, after getting through another day of school, she shifted uncomfortably in her chair. It was challenging trying to study in the café today, but she had to get through her homework at least.

Daniel surprised her by placing a coffee in front of her. She mumbled "thanks", making sure not to look up. She would rather he assume she was focused, not recovering from one of her father's benders. Thinking about last night brought back visions of the woman with scuffed stilettos, not to mention the look of vengeance on her face while she was bent over the couch... Ugh. No. That woman was feral.

Grace inched forward in her chair, hoping for some relief then moved back when she found none. Concentrate on the homework, she murmured. Focus. She just needed to finish this year.

"Are you okay?" Daniel asked quietly. He was still standing at her table.

Grace nodded. She could not let him see her face. Her father's backhand had left a bruise and small cut above her cheek, courtesy of his silver ring. The makeup she applied for school had most likely worn off, and she'd forgotten to grab it when she left. Dad was usually better at delivering blows in places they didn't show. *Blend in*, he always said. But bruises on your face didn't allow you to blend in. Yeah, her dad was losing it.

"Grace?" she heard Daniel whisper. "Grace."

She looked up and seeing the look on Daniel's face, realised she'd zoned out. Shit.

"Oh fu..." Daniel hissed. His gaze shifted from confusion to concern. "What happened?"

Grace moved her hand to her face. "Oh. Nothing. I walked into the door last night. It was really dark. I couldn't see."

"Grace. It was a super moon last night. My house was lit up like a rugby stadium."

"I'm fine. Really." She tried to continue working, but Daniel pulled out a chair and sat. He reached across the table, placing his hand on hers. She snatched it away quickly as if his hand was a live wire.

"Grace. Who did that to you?" Daniel's voice cut her to her core. She could usually deal with her father's moods. But whatever drugs he was now into, things had intensified. She felt lost, unsure of what to do. Her father had gone from being frustrated at their situation to something else. How could she describe it? Rage, for sure, but the loathing toward her was new. Bringing the woman home last night? That was new, too. Grace thought things were looking up. He told her he had a new job. But his incompetence to hold a job was new as well. Normally, he could hold a job down for a few months. Until they ran, at least. Now it had all come to a head. His beatings had intensified. She was used to the occasional beating when he was really pissed off. But not like this, not showing the bruises. And not this often. She'd always been vigilant around her father's anger. She knew what to do to avoid the line of fire. Now it seemed...

"Grace?"

"It's complicated," she whispered.

"Okay. Do you want me to take you home?"

She shook her head. Too fast. It made her dizzy. Still, she couldn't bring herself to meet his eyes.

"Are you safe there, Grace?" The question threw her. Grace slowly looked at him, her eyes revealing an untold story. Slowly, as if the years of hiding were finally too much, she shook her head.

She watched as he opened his mouth and closed it again. Tears formed in her eyes. Daniel reached out for her hand again.

"How can I help? Do you want to go to the police?" Grace shook her head vehemently. The thought of that made her want to throw up. Or maybe admitting her circumstances was what made her feel nauseous. Admitting it made things real. No, she wouldn't involve the police. She just wanted to get out of her situation.

"Okay. What about your boyfriend?" he asked. What? What boyfriend? He was the only guy she'd ever found attractive. Who the hell was he talking about?

"The guy you're always with. Young. Black. Good looking, I guess. I thought you guys were a couple."

"You mean Lowell?" she chuckled, relieved. Her laughter soon filled the café.

"Why are you laughing? You always look, I don't know. Together."

"Oh my God. No," she said. She shook her head, gently this time. "He and I are friends. Just friends. Lowell is gay."

"Oh. Okay. But he's not the one that did that..." he asked. He nodded toward her bruised face. Her hand rose automatically to her cheek.

"No. He's not."

"So...?" She hesitated at answering. Did she want to tell him? Her eyes scanned his. She saw concern. Maybe sympathy, which she hated. Maybe a little pity. She hated that more.

She scanned the surrounding area out of habit. Who else noticed her? She noticed two police officers walking past the café. She put her head down, partially covering her face with her hair. Another habit. She heard Daniel sigh. Her eyes met his, but she kept her head down. She considered him for a few seconds. Could she trust him? Something told her she could. She looked around again. She had to trust her gut.

"They're from my dad," she whispered, then quickly wanted to take the words back. Other than to Lowell, she never talked about her father. She didn't know why. Instinct, she guessed. It was safer not to. So why now? Why this guy? Why Daniel?

"Have you called the cops on him? You know it's..."

Daniel said harshly, then sat back quickly against his chair in exasperation. She felt the hairs on the back of her neck go up. Cautious now, she was confused by his aggressive response to the situation. "Sorry."

"I know what it is. You don't have to tell me. Like I said, it's complicated. It's just until I finish my H.S.C. Then I'm free." Her hand wrapped around the schoolbook in front of her. She clung to it like it was a life preserver. She knew her education was her only way out.

"What can I do? How can I help you?" asked Daniel, leaning in.

Grace looked down. Then, taking a deep breath, she looked directly at Daniel. Did she trust him? She barely knew him.

"I don't know you," she whispered.

"I'm a country boy, getting a double degree in agriculture and business management. I have a part-time job in finance at a small company in the city," he said. He hesitated, then lowered his voice and added, "I just want to be sure you're safe. You don't know me from Adam, but I'm trustworthy. And, well … I've been around this kind of thing before."

Adam? Who the hell was Adam? Now she was really confused. And what did he mean by, 'this kind of thing'? Her defences went up. She moved again in her seat and winced.

"What do you mean by 'this kind of thing'?" she asked curiously, but she seriously needed to move the attention away from herself.

"I had an old girlfriend. Her Dad was... well, she

wasn't safe either. I won't do anything you don't want me to do. I just want to help, and I thought…"

"Well, I'm okay. My Dad has a temper. Usually, I can avoid his moods." She closed her books. She was done with her homework. At least for now. She couldn't focus anymore if she tried. Her head was spinning. She wanted to go home and sleep, to forget about her life for a while. If only she could. Her father and the skanky woman flashed into her mind.

"It's not your fault, you know," Daniel mumbled.

"Yeah, I know," she said, softly.

"You're also not responsible for him. Or his behaviour."

"Yeah, I know that too. I duck and cover when I can," she said, trying to lighten the conversation. Although that was easier before. Now, he seemed more intent on making her life miserable. He was angrier, but she had no clue why and she guessed it related to money. Everything was. Was it more than that? He was certainly more nit-picky lately too. Usually when that happened, they were packing up soon after. Daniel was staring at her. Had she not heard a question?

"I have a plan. Ride it out until the end of the year. Finish my H.S.C. It's the only way… It's why I don't date. No distractions."

"Maybe you should. It would keep you away from home at least?" She saw a flash of interest in his eyes. She hadn't imagined it. Maybe Lowell was right after all. He was smooth. Maybe he was just trying to hook up after all? She sat back and looked at him, long enough to make him squirm. He played with her empty coffee cup on the table. Was he pondering his next move?

"How old are you anyway?" she asked.

"Twenty-one," he answered. She nodded. Not as old as she initially thought. She stared at him. He looked down and spun the coffee cup around in his hands.

"Does your friend, Lowell… does he know about your dad?" he eventually asked.

"Yes. He's sworn that he won't call the police unless I say so."

Daniel nodded. "That's hard, as your friend. I mean, your dad shouldn't be hitting you like that." He stared at her, and she saw a darkness shroud his eyes, like a shield coming down in front of a secret he wasn't willing to share with her. Maybe he was from an abusive home, too? She wanted to reach out to him, take his hand, but she had her own worries. Worrying about Lowell was all she could handle. She sat up a little straighter in her chair, taking on the responsibility of her own truths. Seeing his pain, she made a decision.

"My dad's problem is with drugs and alcohol," she admitted. "He's using but I don't know what. Everything has gotten more frequent. Both the drugs and the slap downs." It was more than that, the voice in her head reminded her. "But I can handle it. I know how to avoid it. Most of the time." She threw her chin out, bolstering her own confidence but knowing her bruises betrayed her.

"Lately, it's been stuff that's caught me by surprise. Like, last night." She reached up and touched her shoulder, feeling the sting once more.

"Why do you stay?" he whispered. "Surely there's somewhere you can go?"

She was quiet for a minute. It was the same question

Lowell asked many times. It was the question she'd been asking herself more often lately, too.

"I don't know," she said eventually. She didn't know. Not really. She tried to explain it. "Because he is my dad? I mean, he hasn't always been this way. I know, deep down, that he cares. He does. I'm sure it's hard to understand and I'm not doing a fabulous job explaining it either…"

Daniel returned to spinning the white ceramic coffee cup in front of him. She couldn't read him. Eventually, he looked up at her.

"Okay. Can I at least give you my phone number?" he asked. "Just in case you need to get out. Or if you need a friend. I know we've just met. But, well, I'd feel better if you had it. It's up to you if you want to delete it or not."

She hesitated. He seemed genuine, and her instincts told her he was okay. Besides, when her dad swapped out the SIM card at the end of the month, like he did every month, Daniel's number would disappear with it. She pulled out her battered old Nokia from her backpack, scrolled through to her contacts, and passed him the phone. He added his number and handed the phone back to her. She had four numbers listed: her father's, Lowell's, work and now Daniel's. She changed his name to D, just in case her father snooped.

He handed her his phone. "Add yours, so I'll answer if you ever decide to contact me."

"You know, this is a weird way to get my number. You could've just asked," she smirked. He chuckled. Typing, she was relieved this number was easy to remember. It was hard to keep track when it was changed every month.

"But would you have given the number to me, if I'd asked?"

"Yeah, probably not," she said, knowing full well she wouldn't have. Lowell's words came back to her. *Be careful, Jelly.*

"I've noticed you turn all those other guys away. What do you say to them? They always hightail it out of here right afterwards."

"What guys?" A chill ran down her back. She'd had a feeling someone was watching her for weeks. Had it been Daniel?

"Shit, I sound like a stalker. I'm really not. It's just that, I've seen how the guys hit on you here. They run for the door, every time, right after they approach you. It was actually pretty entertaining to watch."

"Oh my God," she groaned, "I just tell them I'm studying for my H.S.C. After that, they run faster than I can take my next breath. I guess they're sensible. Unlike you."

"Yeah, well. I'm happy just to get to know you," he said, his blue eyes blazing.

"I think you got the short end of the stick. You've gotten yourself mixed up with some high school girl who gets beaten up by her dad."

10

GRACE LOOKED AROUND. *The walls were close, as if she were in a closet, and they were splattered red. In an instant, everything went pitch black and someone was screaming in the distance. Feeling something cold in her hand, she thought about a phone number she was supposed to dial. The number Mummy told her. Mummy. She had to help Mummy. Confused, she couldn't remember the number. Think. Think. Think.*

"What the fuck?!" Her father's spittle sprayed across her face. His words were muffled, unclear. In her nightmare, she was now a teenager, not the five-year-old she'd been seconds ago. Her father backhanded her, and she fell into the wall. Something hard bit into her shoulder, as it had in her reality only a few nights before.

Dazed, Grace saw blood oozing from the red suitcase. Her father flung the suitcase across the room, scattering the contents across the floor. Clothes, books, a hairdryer, and her 'absolutes' all lay at her feet. She felt the phone in her hands once more. She was five again. The teenager was gone.

. . .

Grace sat up in the cold room, her bed creaking, and wiped away the tears streaming down her cheeks.

"The red suitcase again," she whispered into the blackness. Why that suitcase? Something about it made her think it been her mother's. But the phone? That was new. Maybe the phone was due to her texting Lowell last night, telling him she'd given Daniel her phone number. Yes, that had to be it. She took a deep breath, listening for sounds outside her room. The reassuring silence allowed her to lie back down.

She thought again about moving in with Lowell. She was so tired of living on the edge and these nightmares weren't helping. This, whatever this was, couldn't be normal, could it?

Blend in. Don't bring attention to yourself.

Her father's words rung in her head. She lived by those words, but why would she need to blend in? People on the streets stood out, proud of who they were and what they stood for. She still didn't understand why he was so adamant about it. But there was fear there. His fear. But fear of what? She didn't know. For her, it was fear from her father's wrath. His behaviour lately was so erratic. She knew they were running from something, someone. She wasn't stupid. They'd been running her whole life. The problem was every time she asked, the rare times he'd been sober enough, she'd received a thrashing, verbal or otherwise. So she'd stopped asking. His last words on the subject were 'it's none of your business.' But it was her business, wasn't it? It was her life, too.

Blend in. Don't bring attention to yourself.

Her friendship with Lowell was one thing, but living with a black English guy would certainly bring attention. Could she risk it? She rubbed her hands over her arms, feeling the goosebumps. She was excited about the possibility of gaining freedom. Could she leave without her father knowing? Would he even realise she was gone? She thought about that. At least not for a few days, she thought, if she did it stealthily. Could she stay hidden from him and whatever else they were running from? From her father, maybe. But she didn't know what they were running from, so she couldn't answer that piece. What if he found her? Her father terrified her. She could acknowledge that to herself now. He wasn't the same dad she'd grown up with. Summoning her gumption, she knew that whatever he was involved in, she needed to distance herself from it. She needed to get far, far away.

She needed to talk to Lowell, and soon.

11

WHERE ARE YOU? Lowell's text came through with a distinct buzz.

Almost there, grandpa. Just hang on! she responded. The train was running late and she assumed he was illegally parked. He often was.

+ choc waiting. If you aren't here in 5 mins, I'm eating it.

I'm on the bloody train! Don't eat my chocolate. I'll be there in 10.

She disembarked at Eastwood station and found Lowell leaning against his car in the parking lot. He waved her over.

"Hurry up! I'm going to get a ticket."

"Geez. Okay, okay. God, what's up with you?"

"Shit day. Got an email from my mother. Not good. Come on. Toblerone awaits." Lowell yanked the car door open for her, the hinge screaming in protest. He walked to the driver's side and, when he slammed his door, she jumped.

"Sorry, Jelly," he looked over at her. "John on a roll again? That bruise is new," he whistled. Then he looked up into his rear vision mirror and turned the ignition.

"It's okay. What's happened with you?" Grace asked, changing the subject, putting her seat belt on. Pain blasted through her shoulder.

"Dad happened," he said, putting the car in gear. "He found out that Mum's been meeting me once a month. So, he showed her how unhappy he was with that piece of information. With his fists." He looked over his shoulder to check for an opening in the oncoming traffic, then darted out into the flow. "She emailed to tell me she couldn't meet with me next week. Geezus, Grace. I don't know if I should go home to help Mum, or just call the cops. The thing is, I know they won't do anything about it. Dad is in deep with some of those boys. Has been ever since we moved to Australia ten years ago. Pays to be a corrupt politician, I guess. Maybe I should just wait until things settle down?"

"What does your gut say?" she asked, gripping the seat as he rounded the traffic circle too fast.

"Right now, go home and beat the shit out of him. But that would only make it worse for Mum. And I know that's my anger talking, not my gut. I don't know what to do at this point."

"Is your mum alright?" Grace was relieved when they stopped at a red light. When he navigated the curves, her seat belt kept locking, which wasn't helping her discomfort at all. But she didn't want to tell Lowell how to drive, either.

"Yeah, she is," he said, after taking a moment. He

looked over at her in the passenger seat. "Thanks for asking me that."

"Why wouldn't I? She's your mum. She's the person you love most in the world. Is she going to leave your dad? I mean, she has choices," she said, too quickly. She wasn't surprised when Lowell shot her a look, one he had given her a million times before. The one that read: *So do you.*

"You know, I wish she would. But she won't. She's too afraid of the repercussions," he said. They were silent for the five-minute drive to his apartment. Lowell pulled into the parking garage underneath the building, parked his car, and jerked the handbrake in frustration.

"Now, grab that bag at your feet, Jelly, and let's go and overindulge in chocolate."

They walked up to the second floor, and he unlocked the heavy steel door, holding it open for her. Grace walked through and dropped her battered backpack beside his couch and carefully sat down. Lowell threw his keys on to the console table and collapsed onto his faded blue loveseat.

"What's the latest about the café guy? You got his number, you said? That's new for you." Lowell reached into the bag Grace carried from the car and pulled out two Toblerone bars, tossing one to her. She caught it, mid-air.

"Thanks!"

"Of course. So? Details please," he said, unwrapping his chocolate.

"He..." she didn't want to admit that Daniel knew about her latest beating. She was usually so careful about that, as Lowell well knew, but she had no other way to explain it.

"He asked about the bruise on my face," she said. Lowell raised his eyebrow. "After he bought me a coffee," she added.

"Well, I will say nothing about someone else supporting your coffee habit. So, what did you say when he asked about the bruise?" Lowell asked, popping a chocolate triangle into his mouth.

"Um, I told him I walked into a door since it was really dark, and I couldn't see. Except that I forgot it was a super moon that night. Everything was really bright."

"That's not like you," he said, concern lacing his tone. "You're usually good at covering John's indiscretions. But then, he's usually pretty good about where he strikes. And you're babying your shoulder. What's with that?" Damn, she'd hoped he wouldn't notice.

"I have a cut on it. Where I hit the chest of drawers."

"Have you treated it?" She shook her head. All she had at home was toilet paper, so she'd used that to stop the bleeding on her shoulder. Lowell got up from the couch and headed to his bathroom. She thought about his comment of her slipping up.

Lowell returned with some antiseptic cream and alcohol swabs.

"I guess I got sloppy, just as my dad is lately," she said. "That's what I wanted to talk to you about."

She pulled her shirt down enough to show Lowell the cut and noticed his face go dark with anger. She hated adding to his worries, especially since his mother was dealing with the same thing.

"Geezus, Jelly." He got up and went back into his bathroom. She heard him rattle around in his medicine cabinet and came back out with a handful of supplies.

"This has got to stop. He's going to kill you one day," he said, tossing butterfly bandages and more alcohol swabs into her lap. The aggressiveness made her jump.

"Sorry. Guess I'm just fed up with fucked-up bullies beating on their loved ones," he said and turned her to inspect her shoulder in better light. Facing away from him made it easier for her to plunge forward with her question.

"I know. That's what I wanted to talk to you about. I keep asking myself why I stay. I guess I don't know anymore. You've asked me that and Daniel asked me the same question too. Last night, I had the nightmare I've been having for months now. It's like my brain is trying to tell me something, but I don't know what. I can't sleep anymore because of them. They're horrible. And I know I don't have enough money but…" She sucked in her breath when she felt a burning sensation explode over her shoulder.

"Sorry Jelly, I don't mean to hurt you. Look, I've said it before. Move in here. It's small, but you can have my room. I'll sleep on the couch." She scowled at him. No, she didn't want that. She didn't want to put him out. "Don't worry, it pulls out into a bed. We'll make it work."

"I feel so bad Lowell. Asking you… asking for help."

"You said my mum has choices," he said as he squeezed some antiseptic cream into his fingers. "So do you. This is yours. Stay. It's better than ending up dead."

"Thank you. I was going to ask if it was okay if I stayed just a little while. I'll find a place soon…" His fingers gently spread the antiseptic cream across her wound.

"Stay as long as you want," he said as he applied the bandage. "Really. Throw in whatever you can for the groceries, and we'll call it even."

"I'm just scared he'll find me," she whispered. He pulled her shirt back up.

"Does he know about me? About our friendship?" She shook her head. Of that, she was sure.

"Then you should be okay. Maybe take the long way home from school for a couple of weeks, just in case. I'm sure you don't want to change schools at this late stage, since you only have, what? Five months left?"

"Four," she said. "And no. I'd rather stay and finish the year."

"Then we'll take precautions. Maybe Daniel can help you with that, too. You know, give you lifts here and there…" She gaped at him, stunned at the suggestion.

"I'm teasing Jelly. Although it would be good for you to date."

"I don't need the distraction. You know I don't date," she replied, and unwrapped her chocolate when he got up to wash his hands in the kitchen. He came back in, wiping his hands on a tea towel.

"Girl, you're not dead. If you don't want to date him, then just sleep with him, and get it over with. Then you can move on and go back to your studies."

"No. I…. I can't do that," she looked up at him and added, "I'm not a slut."

"No, you're not. But the fun you are missing out on! I'm not saying give it out to every guy you meet! But he sounds hot and if you like him, then…"

"I do. Like him, I mean," she stumbled over her words.

"I just don't want to get involved. I have enough on my plate."

"Just take it slow. Trust your instincts," he said, dropping another Toblerone wedge into his mouth. "Only you know what you're ready for. But Jelly, the world really is a lovely place. People are kind if you open yourself up to them. I know you're scared. I would be if I had your dad. He's a lot like mine in his bullish ways. Yes, it will take some adjustment. But Jelly, once you're away from him, you'll have freedom like never before. Trust me on that. You'll see."

12

"WHAT THE FUCK took you so long?" Her father's gravelly voice greeted her, when she opened the front door two nights later. The place was as dark as the night outside and it felt icy cold.

She opened the door further, allowing the hall light to illuminate the room. Her father was slouched on the futon in the far corner, the balcony's sliding glass door wide open.

"I had work," she said, pausing a minute longer at the front door.

"More like whoring around."

"What? No. I'm turning the light on," she said and flipped the switch. Turning, she gasped. The apartment had been turned upside down. A shiver went down her spine. She slowly closed the door, regretting it the minute she heard the metallic thud. What the hell happened in here? The two dining chairs were upended, the table pushed against the wall. The garbage bin was lying on its side, its contents littering the floor. There were cups and dishes all over the kitchen counter, but they looked clean. She had to find out what happened, but was too afraid to ask. Did this mean they were moving again? Had her father done this? Or someone else?

"Who the fuck is Daniel?" he barked, getting to his feet. He unsteadily moved toward her. She stepped backwards, her back hitting the front door.

"What?" she stammered, feeling the blood drain from her face.

"Daniel. Who's Daniel? I found this… in your room." He threw a piece of paper at her, hitting her shoulder before it fell to the floor. She picked it up. It was the note Daniel wrote when she'd first met him. God, he was just buying her coffee.

"Where did you find this?" she asked, knowing full well she'd hidden it in her bottom drawer, buried amongst some school papers.

"I told you, in your room. I was looking for my money."

"What money?"

"The hundred dollars in my wallet yesterday. It's not there today, so I went looking for it. It's my house, I can look wherever I want. Now, who the fuck is Daniel?"

She stayed silent.

"What's the matter? Are you knocked up? Your whore of a mother got knocked up. Had to marry her." He walked back toward the couch but stumbled over its edge. In frustration, he kicked the edge of the milk crate the television sat on. The TV crashed to the floor. Shattered glass littered the floor like broken memories.

"Fuck," he slurred. He turned back to her.

"So, you're now a whore. Just like her. Are you pregnant?"

"What? No." Grace walked quickly toward her bedroom. She needed to escape. She needed to get her things and get out. Now.

"Why not? Like mother, like daughter."

"Dad. Don't say that. It's not true," she said, standing halfway between the table and her bedroom, dumbfounded.

"How would you know? You don't even remember her." Fear made her freeze when he staggered toward her.

I do, she thought. I remember her.

"So, tell me. Do you string them along like your mother did? Make them beg for it? Keep them panting at your heels? Or is this, this Daniel guy… is he your pimp? Maybe that's it? Are you turning tricks? Is this your way to hook them? Maybe that's why you're home late."

"No. I was working. Really." She picked at her nails, her cuticles. She traced the ravaged edges and picked, feeling the skin slicing back.

"Then where's my hundred dollars? It was in my wallet yesterday."

"I don't know. I don't have it."

"Like hell you don't. You've taken whatever money you want before. Who else would take it?"

"I don't know." Although she guessed it was some other junkie he hung out with. She stripped more skin around her nail beds. She was panicked. She felt the wetness from blood seeping out from her cuticles as she picked, picked, picked at them.

"Fucking liar. That's what you are." He rushed toward her and caught her by the throat, slamming her against the wall.

"Where is it? Where's my fucking money?"

"I don't know," she gasped. She wrapped her hands around his wrists, trying to pull his hands away from her neck. He threw her to the side and her injured shoulder slammed into the doorframe of her bedroom. She teetered but stayed upright. The wound reopened with the impact, and she felt warm blood running down her back.

"Where the fuck is it?" he bellowed.

He came at her again, swinging. This time, she ducked, retreating into the lounge room. She spun around, then stepped back. She needed to get out, flee. Grace reached down to grab her backpack by the table when her father caught her chin with a right hook. She flew backward onto the couch. Sprawled out, he grabbed her hair and yanked her down hard, his mouth foaming.

"Where the fuck is it, you whore?"

"I don't have it! I didn't take it. But you can have the money in my wallet," she begged. He yanked her back up with a fist full of hair. She was tall, but he was taller. Grace reached her arms out in defence, and her father caught one arm and twisted it behind her. She heard the pop. She wanted to scream, but he swung again and caught her hard in the right kidney. This time, her scream came. Where were the neighbours? Why weren't they helping her? Surely, they could hear what was going on in this apartment? Her father tossed her forward, and she flew straight for the table. She reached out and caught herself on the edge, narrowly missing her head as she fell.

She lay helpless on the floor. She tried to grab her backpack, but her father snatched it from her.

"Oh no," she whimpered, although too quietly for her father to hear. "Please, no." She couldn't afford for him to find her treasures. She almost cried in relief when he pulled out her wallet, dropping her backpack to the floor. She had thirty dollars tucked inside of it. Money she was going to add to the secret pocket in her backpack. He whipped out the cash and threw the wallet back at her, landing it squarely in her face.

"Well, that's a deposit on what you stole," he said as he plunged the cash into his jeans pocket. "I'll expect the rest tomorrow." He left the apartment, slamming the door behind him.

Grace whimpered, afraid to move. After a moment, she slowly stood, grimacing with every movement.

She retrieved her things and stumbled to her bedroom. The room was turned upside down. John hadn't just gone through her drawers, he'd ripped through her mattress, broken her cell phone charger, and ripped her school uniform, most likely trying to get into the pocket in his rage. Grace stood at the door. She stared vacantly into the space, emotionally stripped bare. Tears welled and tumbled down her cheeks. It was all she could do. She felt completely broken.

13

IT HAD BEEN a hell of a week. She was still in agony from the too-frequent beatings. The last one resulted in a dislocated shoulder. She heard the pop when her father wretched her arm, giving her no choice but to go to the medical centre to pop it back in. She told the staff she'd been thrown from a horse. Somehow, they believed her. She'd seen horse farms when she'd driven around with Lowell, so she figured it was a valid excuse.

Her father had not been home since that night. At least, not when she was there. The television remained broken on the floor; glass still scattered around it. She left it that way, along with the rest of the mess around the apartment. He made the mess. He could clean it up for once.

Now it was Thursday afternoon and she'd just left Lowell after hanging out at his yoga studio. The place still smelled like fresh paint. They'd talked about her situation again. Lowell urged her to move in immediately, but she needed to get out of her father's place without him suspecting. And she needed to make it to her eighteenth birthday before she moved out, so there'd be no 'minor' strings her father could pull. She wanted to tell Lowell it was her birthday tomorrow, but she kept that information to herself. Birthdays weren't a big deal anymore. Not since her mother died. Turning eighteen meant nothing more to her than legally becoming an adult. As for the rest? She hadn't had a birthday celebration in years, so why change that now?

Heading to work, the near empty train to Macquarie Centre rocked her into a zone. She gazed out the window into the blurred suburbs, watching the world rush by with the speed of the train. Grace went through her exit plan for the umpteenth time. She was set.

When she finally looked beyond the seats before her, an old man sat at the end of the carriage. The scowled look on his face screamed: 'Leave me alone!', his hands clenched around the daily newspaper. Wrinkles creased his eyes, his mouth turned down, and his brow seemed to be in a perpetual frown. When the train stopped at the next station, a young mother boarded with her little girl in a stroller, taking a seat in the same section as the old man. The little girl, dressed in polka dot leggings and a long shirt, wore her hair up in a high pigtail. She exuded sunshine and happiness. She peered around the stroller at the old man and wiggled her fingers at him, her voice squeaking out a perky hello.

His face lit up, turning Mr. Hyde into Dr. Jekyll. The expression on the gentleman's face removed twenty years from his age, especially when he began playing peekaboo with the little girl. He laughed when she giggled, the sound of his laughter booming through the carriage. The transformation of the man caught Grace completely by surprise, making her laugh out loud.

Grace tried to remember if she had a grandfather. Was he at all like this man? Had she ever been like this little girl, full of life and wonder? Those memories were hard to remember now. Even her memories of Nanny were distorted, but she remembered love whenever she thought of her. Where was she? Had she looked for her? Grace turned to look out the window again. She sighed. She'd never know about her grandparents now, and she couldn't ask her father. Not now. She needed to stop thinking about the past and get on with her future.

At nine-thirty that night, Grace closed her till and hugged her boss Sue goodbye. She loved working with Sue. She had a dry sense of humour most didn't pick up on, and a generous nature she only dished out to her favourites. Sue shared she was her favourite of all of them and was devastated Grace was leaving. But Grace needed to work closer to Lowell's. Well, that was mostly true. The reality was her father knew where she worked. She couldn't risk him finding her there. She'd applied at two supermarkets closer to Lowell's, and Sue had called them both, providing Grace with a high commendation. She was very thankful for that.

Walking home with the throng of other workers, Grace mentally went through what she needed to pack. She would leave the apartment behind when she left for school in the morning. There was very little she wanted, and it all fit easily into her duffel. Her 'absolutes', her precious few trinkets, were buried in her school backpack and her cash tucked in the special pocket she'd sewn into it. That was really all she needed. The rest was replaceable, but she knew she'd need some other basics.

With her mind on her mental checklist, she unlocked the front door and the stench almost knock her over. The place reeked of alcohol, body odour, and that smell she still could not place. Her stomach lurched and, before realising her mistake, she let the door thud behind her. Her father staggered out of his bedroom, anger pouring out of him like hot lava.

One more day. Just one more day. With her chin up and backpack firmly over her shoulder, she walked boldly toward her room, but at her door, her father's hand clenched around her forearm.

"One more day," she whispered, so quietly no one could have heard.

"What the fuck did you say?" he growled, but he let her go.

"Nothing. Just mumbling to myself," she said and moved toward the door, intending to close it, but her father's hand was on the doorframe.

"Just like your fucking mother. She used to do that shit all the time. Mumble, mumble, mumble."

"It was nothing, Dad. Just mumbling about school."

"Think you're better than the rest of us, huh? Little Miss Superior? Well, you're not. You know that, right? I went to fucking university. I even had a successful business. A landscape designer. Then it all went to shit. Just like that." He went to click his fingers, but he was too loaded to make them connect.

"I know, Dad. You told me."

"You don't know shit," he spat. "Do you even know what happened? Do you?"

"No," she whispered, fearing the answer, but needing it all the same.

"Let me tell you what happened. Your fucking grandparents." Grace's mind went back to the old man on the train.

"They fucking ruined me. And your grandmother? Hated me from the moment she met me. She was a fucking bitch. Fucking *meddling* bitch. Thought she was better than everyone else. Hated her little princess marrying the likes of me, even though I was far more successful than her darling daughter. Nope, she hated me the moment she laid eyes on me."

"I didn't know. Where are they?"

"What?" His pupils narrowed as they tried to focus on her face. His head swayed.

"Where are my grandparents now?" she asked softly, regretting the question as soon as it passed her lips. But something nagged at her. A memory.

"Who gives a shit? She got hers. I showed her. Fucking cow, meddling with me. She had no right."

"Showed her what?" Grace whispered. An icy chill filled her.

"Nothing. She's a fucking bitch. She deserved nothing..." He stumbled back to the lounge room, grabbed his beer and took a long swig. He swayed for a minute, then turned back to Grace with hatred in his eyes.

"She knew her daughter was a fucking whore. She just never wanted to see it. And who did she blame? Me. She knew her daughter was a cokehead. She knew she slept with any guy who'd buy her what she wanted. Yeah, she knew. But who did she blame? Me. Well, she got hers!" He tried to walk back toward his room, but his legs weren't moving properly. He grabbed the edge of the chair.

"Dad…" He turned and gaped at her. She opened her mouth to say more, but there was something in his eyes that scared the shit out of her. Her gut told her to shut up. She studied her ravaged cuticles. She wanted to pick at them but controlled herself.

"What? What?! God, you're like her. Take it wherever you can get it. Just like your mother. Probably a fucking whore, too. Are you? Do you sleep with anything that turns his head your way? Fucking useless you are. Should have left you behind. You've only ever been a fucking anchor. I could have gone places, done things, but noooo. Had to drag you around. Well, you're nearly done with school, right? Yeah. Nearly. Yeah, good. Good fucking riddance to you then." He stood there, swaying, nodding his head, living in his own mental universe while Grace stood at the door of her room, feeling faint.

"Yeah, you're exactly like her. A whore. That's all you'll ever be. Just like your mother." Then he turned on his heel and walked out the front door, letting it slam behind him.

Grace stood at her bedroom door, her mouth open. The words stung. He'd called her a whore plenty of times. That didn't bother her. She knew the truth. But the words about her mum? Those words cut. She barely remembered her mother. Only snippets. Everything about her mother was good. She was always hugging Grace. Telling her she loved her, always playing fun games with her, like the tea parties they had with her dolls, and running around the house, playing hide and seek. Suddenly Grace remembered words. Words an older woman had said. Was it her Nanny? Oh, my God. Yes. It was her grandmother. She remembered the woman clearly now. And the words she remembered made Grace's knees buckle.

'Come home to me, sweetness. You'll be safe here.'

Grace's mind went immediately to a red suitcase, like the one always in her nightmares. But this time, she remembered it in a different place. The red suitcase was her mother's suitcase, and that suitcase was sitting by the front door of their house. The suitcase was real. Shit.

Grace was already awake and dressed by the time her alarm went off the following morning. She was packed and ready to go, her duffel in the far back corner under her bed. The last thing she needed was her father to see the packed bag. Today was the day, her eighteenth birthday. She'd barely slept, she was so excited. She thought of her mum.

Her mind jumped at her grandmother's words: *'Come home to me, sweetness. You'll be safe here.'*

Had her mother been in trouble? In danger? Was her father abusive to her as well? Was there something more to her dreams? She shook her head. She needed to focus. Now was her opportunity to get out.

She opened her bedroom door a fraction. She hadn't heard her father return all night. Still, she needed to be careful. She stood completely still, listening for sounds of his presence. It was quiet. All she could hear was the cacophony of cars caught up in the morning commute. She stepped out into the hallway and poked her head around to see into her father's bedroom. Empty. She tiptoed further into the lounge room. Empty as well. She exhaled, then turned into the bathroom.

She brushed her teeth then washed her face, going gently around the cut above her cheek, slowly healing. Grabbing some concealer from the lone drawer, she dabbed some liquid on the faded bruising, then pulled her hair up into a ponytail. Her shoulder was still painful, but she ploughed ahead. When she was done, she stopped, and giving herself the treasured moment, she smiled into the cracked mirror.

"Happy Birthday," she whispered. "Freedom is your gift."

Without wanting to push her luck, she grabbed her toothbrush and the few toiletries she had and returned to her room. Fighting through the physical misery from her injuries, she put her boots on, then, got down on all fours and pulled the bag out from under her bed. She tossed the toiletries into the bag and took one last look around. There was nothing else.

When she walked by the kitchen table, she looked toward the notepad sitting on top of the bar fridge. There was a pen lying beside it. She paused, thought of what she'd write if she left a note. Grace knew it would be only one word: goodbye. She wasn't sad or angry. She was resigned to the fact that John killed any reason for her to stay. Her father was long gone.

Walking out the door, leaving the notepad blank, she hitched her duffel up over her shoulder and took in her first breath of freedom.

14

Grace's phone buzzed. With her schoolbooks open all around her on Lowell's queen-sized bed, she leaned over and picked it up from the small wooden bedside table.

Hey Grace. Are you okay? I haven't seen you in a few weeks.

She was shocked to see the text from Daniel. She'd forgotten about him since moving in with Lowell. For the last two weeks, she'd been avoiding her phone, dreading the inevitable call from her father, asking where she was. The constant worry consumed her. Daniel's text was a pleasant surprise, but she didn't know how to respond.

Looking around the room, thinking of her response, she realised this room was everything she dreamed of only weeks before. The big comfortable bed, the linens that kept her warm. There was even a tree-lined street outside her window. She felt… numb. She knew from experience this could all go away any minute. She felt like she was in a dream, waiting for her dad to walk through the door and drag her back to reality. She was lucky Lowell offered her a place to stay. She didn't want to go back to the life of living out of a car or in a cold, mouldy apartment. Lowell insisted she stay as long as she wanted, but she felt guilty. She was living someone else's life, not her own.

She caressed the bedcovers, felt their softness. A tree swaying in the breeze outside drew her attention, its leaves sparkling from the sunlight. She was lucky. Too lucky. Looking back down at her phone, she understood Daniel was part of that dream life fantasy too. He seemed too good to be true. Her fingers hovered over the keys before finding the words.

Hi Daniel. Yeah, I'm good. I moved in w/ Lowell. Things are better.

She placed the phone back on the table, but the buzz was immediate. She picked it up again.

Oh good. Will I see u at the café soon?

Not likely, she thought. She doubted she'd ever go back there again. It was too close to her father's apartment.

No. Sorry.

This time she waited for a response, although she wasn't too sure there'd be one. Soon enough though, she could see the text dots start, then stop. Pause. Then start and stop again. She returned the phone to the table. She felt bad, but she needed to be cautious. Since her father knew about Daniel from the note, seeing him was an enormous risk. She was shocked her father never found out about Lowell. At least she hoped he hadn't. She went back to her essay. It was due tomorrow. The phone buzzed again.

Do you wanna see a movie on Sat? As friends. No pressure.

How did she respond to that? She'd never been to a movie before, not that she could remember, anyway. What would it be like? And was this a date? He said as friends. She felt … sad about that. Did she want to go on a date with him? She liked him. A lot. She felt nervous around him, giddy even. It would be nice, she mused. Maybe it was one-sided? Maybe he didn't like her that way? Maybe he was like one of the usual guys at the café? The idea of that hurt even more. She didn't think so. He didn't seem like a player. And the chemistry between them was heady. Besides, he was asking her to a movie. Maybe he did like her? Lowell warned her to be careful. But then, sleep with him, get it over with, then go back to your studies. She was eighteen now. Technically, she was an adult. Not that it mattered. She could go out with a guy if she wanted to. Except… She looked around at her books and knew she had to focus. Her mantra remained, even though she'd thrown out the timing. Dots blinked on the phone again.

Just want to make sure you're ok. Really, no pressure. Just let me know by Friday.

Ah, but she'd have a new SIM card by Friday. She'd been waiting for her first pay cheque from her new job at Coles. With a new SIM card, she'd lose his number and he would no longer have hers. She wouldn't have her father's number either. She'd be glad of that, although he'd probably changed his by now. Still, it was one more step away from the past. She grabbed her school diary, flipped to the back page, and wrote both Lowell and Daniel's numbers down. She'd keep Daniel's number. Just in case.

Okay. I'll let you know.

She paused before pushing send. It sounded cold. She didn't want to… what? Tease him? Was her father right? Was she a whore? Was she stringing him along? Keeping him… what was it that her father said? Panting at my heels? No. No, she wasn't like that. She added *Thanks* and hit send.

An hour later, she heard the front door open and habitually froze. She didn't hear a key in the door. Was it her father? Had he found her? Hearing footsteps, she leapt off the bed and ducked behind the door. She knew her books were a giveaway, but at least she'd have time to react.

"Hey, Jelly. You home?" Lowell's voice rang out like a bird on a beautiful spring day. She released her breath. Of course, it was Lowell. It was his apartment. She was just the squatter. Yes, she was trying to relax about her circumstances, but it would take a while not to react every time the front door opened. She stepped out from behind the door and walked into the small lounge room. Lowell was dressed casually in worn jeans, a Van Morrison t-shirt, and sneakers. Heading into the kitchen, he carried several overflowing grocery bags, his biceps bulging from the load. She followed him into the kitchen, realising his t-shirt was one she'd not seen before. He had a secret hoard of band t-shirts, something she'd never picked up on before.

"Hi," she said. "Wow, what did you buy? Lowell…"

"I have a craving for a chicken tikka, so I'm making one tonight. Hope you're hungry." Lowell was feeding her copious amounts of food since she'd moved in, even sending her off to school each day with a packed lunch.

She'd never had someone do that for her before. She was lucky if she had a peanut butter sandwich, but since schools banned those, it was usually just an apple. Not anymore. Lowell made sure of that.

"What's a... chicken tikka?" she asked, opening the fridge, placing the milk inside.

"Wait. Are you telling me you've never had chicken tikka before?" he asked, pausing to place a gigantic bag of rice in the pantry. Her eyes bulged at the size. It must have cost him a fortune. She had to give him some money. He couldn't afford to support her, and she didn't expect him to, either.

"Um no. I've never heard of it. And Lowell, I will give you money to help pay for all this. I'm so sorry. It's got to have cost you..."

"Stop Jelly. Really, you need to stop apologising. You've been saying sorry all bloody week. It's getting old." He stood staring at her, holding a new pepper grinder in his left hand. She nodded and reflexively picked at her cuticles. He gently squeezed her hand to comfort her. He knew her anxious habit.

"It's nothing to worry about, Jelly. Anyway, Chicken tikka is like, an English staple. Like Aussies and their Thai takeaways. Or their pizzas. And, this is my treat because I have a surprise. We're celebrating."

"Oh?" He handed her a loaf of bread, which she placed in the cupboard above her head. Its usual spot, she'd discovered. Everything had its place in Lowell's apartment.

"Yes. I got a new client today. Well, a group of them, I suppose. It's a group of mums who want to do more than sit in cafes, drinking coffee. They call themselves the 'Bubs and Bubbles' group. They want to bring in one of their nannies, or their babysitter, whatever. Someone else who will look after the babies while the mums do yoga."

"Wow, that's great!" she said, although she had no clue what a babysitter was. Bringing along a grandmother, or a Nanny like hers, to look after a bunch of babies all on her own just seemed… wrong. Still, she was genuinely happy for him. He'd been pitching his yoga studio for weeks.

"Yeah, I've gotten three contracts just this week from a notice I placed in the community paper. And this one is for six months. I think you've brought me luck! So, we're having my all-time favourite for dinner."

Lowell leaned over and grabbed the chopping board and started prepping dinner. She didn't know what he was cooking, but he seemed excited about it. She was happy to eat anything he was making. Turned out, Lowell was a skilled cook. He'd taken cooking lessons with an ex-lover when he was nineteen. The guy didn't stick, but the cooking lessons had. "Are you still going with your homework? Because I'm good to go here. You can set the couch when we're ready to eat. I'd say set the table, but um…" She laughed. He didn't have a table.

"I just have an essay to finish. I'll come help when I'm done. It won't take long."

"Then go finish. Dinner will be ready in about an hour," he said, slicing the package of chicken breasts open.

She walked back to the bedroom, but she could hear everything he was doing in the kitchen. He talked to himself while he cooked, as if he was presenting with a running commentary. When she first moved in, she initially thought someone else was in the apartment and it freaked her out. She'd poked her head out. Seeing no one there, she asked who he was talking to. Remembering his blush, she smiled. Recovering, he admitted he liked to pretend he had his own cooking show and had forgotten she was there. She found it calming now.

Lowell's apartment was cosy. It was barely big enough for one, but they were making it work. She loved living here. Leafy trees were visible outside every window, which was a lovely change from the damp concrete complex she'd lived in before. Lowell was fastidious about keeping the place tidy, a welcome change from her previous life. His obsession with cobalt blue was something that amused her. Almost everything around the place was cobalt blue. The neighbours, a young couple with a baby, were nice too. They apologised for their baby's crying at night almost daily, but Grace barely noticed. She felt safe here. And yet, she waited for the proverbial shoe to drop.

Lowell had offered her his bedroom when she'd moved in, insisting he take the couch. His mother bought him a sofa bed when he found the apartment, hoping to come and stay with him, but his father wouldn't allow it. When Lowell was sixteen, he'd come out to his parents. His father had gone ballistic, almost killing him. His mother rang 000 for an ambulance, after his father stormed out of the house. Afraid he'd return to finish Lowell off, she put him in the ambulance. Alone. The next day, sporting her own black eye, she dropped a bag, full of Lowell's things, at the hospital. She'd tucked money into the inside pocket and told him not to come home until it was safe. Except it never was. His father disowned

Lowell and wouldn't allow him any contact with his mother. But they kept in touch through a secret email account and discretely met at a halfway point in Port Macquarie.

She and Lowell had connected like only survivors could. She still worried that her father would find her. It was bad before, but he could make it much, much worse. She was still looking over her shoulder, and she worried about the repercussions every minute of every day.

"Hey Jelly? I'm heading to the chemist after dinner. You said you needed something? Want to go with?"

"Yes, please," she called back. His cooking commentary continued.

Lowell called out to her an hour later, just as she finished the essay. He heaped their cobalt blue bowls with the curry, adding flat bread to a side plate for each of them. The aroma was intoxicating. She wouldn't fit into her school uniform if she kept eating at this rate. Lowell was so skinny, and she was amazed at how much he ate. He told her he was replenishing calories for swimming and doing yoga, when she commented on the amount of food he served the first week. For her, he was simply making up for her borderline starvation.

"Heard from that guy at the café lately?" he asked, handing her a bowl. Odd, she thought, that he would ask. Was he spying on her? Reading her texts? No, that was just paranoia. Lowell wasn't like that. Not like her father.

"Actually yes. He texted me this afternoon while I was studying," she said, and took a bite. It was spicy, but not overly so.

"And?" he prodded, talking around his full mouth.

"What is this dish called again? It's so good. Thank you."

"Yeah? Good. Chicken tikka with naan. But don't change the subject."

"He asked if I'd be going back to the café soon, since I haven't been since…"

"Yeah," he said, in a worried tone. "Will you?"

He already expressed his concern about her returning to her dad. It was a story he'd heard many times. Friends, people he knew, sometimes returned to abusive homes. She was more worried that her dad would find her. Maybe that was why Lowell had been spoiling her? To keep her living with him, so she'd be out of harm's way. It was certainly working. She'd never had such luxury.

"No, I won't go back there. It's too…"

"Dangerous," he finished for her. She nodded.

"He asked me to a movie. This Saturday. As friends," and took a bite of the delicious naan. She suspected it was something else he'd made himself.

"Are you going?"

Grace had been thinking about it since she got the text, wavering back and forth on the idea. It was risky. Her father knew Daniel existed, but he didn't know what he looked like. She knew where her father hung out. If they avoided that area, they'd be okay.

"Earth to Jelly," said Lowell, scooping some of his Tikka on the flatbread.

"I don't know. I haven't decided," she responded. By now, her bowl was still half full, but she couldn't eat anymore. Lowell's bowl was almost empty.

"Why are you hesitating? Go out with him," he said,

wiping the bottom of his bowl with his bread. "He's hot, you said. He's clearly interested. Friends, yeah, whatever. It would still be good for you to get out. You need to move on with your life, Jelly. Life is exciting. You have so much in front of you."

"We'll see."

15

WHEN THEY ARRIVED at Chemist Warehouse, Grace was surprised to see the place so busy at nine o'clock at night. Lowell grabbed a basket and went in search of his own needs. He found her in the hair colour aisle.

"What are you buying?" said Lowell, standing at her elbow.

"Hair colour," she said, popping it into the basket.

"Wait. That's your normal hair colour," he said, picking up the box clearly stating: 'chestnut brown'. Grace absent-mindedly shook her head.

"It's not? Then what's your natural colour?" he said, flipping the box over then looking up at her.

"Blonde. Light blonde," she replied and continued slowly to the deodorant aisle.

"Jelly. Wait. Why are you colouring it? Blonde would look gorgeous on you."

"Because I can't," she replied. What if that caused John to find her?

She turned and was surprised to see confusion on Lowell's face. Why was he confused? She'd always coloured her hair. Why was he questioning it?

"Who the hell says you can't?" Lowell responded abruptly.

"Because I'm not allowed to be blonde. As soon as the blonde shows, I have to cover it up."

"Is this a John thing?" he asked quietly. Oh shit. What had she just done? She wasn't thinking. She nodded slowly. "How long have you coloured it?"

She didn't answer.

"Jelly, why is he making you colour your hair?"

She'd not shared everything with Lowell in the year she'd known him. He knew about the beatings, her father's temper, but she hadn't told him they were on the run. It wasn't until they'd reached Sydney that they stopped moving so much. Sydney was a good place to hide, her father said. People were everywhere. Small towns made you stand out.

"Jelly? What's going on? What aren't you telling me?"

Grace held a steaming cup of tea after settling into Lowell's comfy blue couch. She agonised over how much she should reveal. She began to speak, then promptly closed her mouth. She owed him the truth. He needed to understand the risk by taking her in. If he thought it was too much, she knew she'd be okay, but she also sensed he would stick by her no matter what. He wasn't the type to back off from anything. Reflexively, she pulled a loose strand of her chestnut brown hair over the scar on her forehead.

"So, what's with the hair colour?" he asked gently. He knew her well enough to know when she was hesitating.

"My hair has always been coloured. I only know I'm blonde because that's the colour that comes through. My Dad used to do it, but I started doing it myself, I don't know, about four years ago? My Dad usually cuts my hair too but never short."

"But why, Jelly?" Lowell took a sip of his tea. She followed suit. The chamomile tea was still hot, but cool enough to sip.

"I don't know…" she wasn't sure how to tell him. She took another sip, trying to find the words. Lowell waited patiently.

"My Dad would always tell me I had to blend in. And, that it hurt him to see me blonde because I looked so much like my mother." Lowell looked thoughtful.

"I think you'd look amazing as a blonde," he said, to fill the silence. She nodded. She wasn't so sure, but she remembered her mother's hair. It was beautiful, like golden sand. Was her hair that colour too?

"What else does he make you do?" he asked.

"Swap out my SIM card on my phone every month, but you know that already," she responded. She'd told him it was because her dad shopped around for phone plans. But that wasn't the reason.

"I do remember one thing he asked me to do, when I was about seven or eight. It was all in line with our, um, big adventure. He said we'd run out of money and needed to get creative. We were moving, coming back to the mainland on the ferry from Tasmania. Before we boarded, we pulled into a parking lot at a park nearby. He told me to go to the toilet because it would be awhile before I could go again. I didn't think anything of it. He liked to drive long distances without stopping. But, when I returned from the toilet, he'd moved stuff around in the campervan. He told me I would get to stay in the van all night but I had to hide under the seat until we were boarded and sailing. I thought it was pretty funny. He gave me a bottle of water and a box of crackers. Oh, and an apple. So, I got in and laid down under the bench seats. We used it for storage. He put the seat cushions over me and said I could take the cushion off overnight, but to have it back on before we docked. I wasn't allowed to get up and move around, just move the cushion, he said. Eventually, he told me to just go to sleep, and we'd be back in Melbourne before I knew it. But under no circumstances was I to get out of the van until we were off the boat."

"Geezus Jelly," hissed Lowell.

"I thought it was a big adventure. Like I was a stowaway. I was reading those kinds of books at the time, so my dad made it a game for me."

"What else?" Grace looked at Lowell, lost in the memory, her lips curled in a gentle smile. "What else did he say you have to do?"

Minutes passed. Grace knew she was taking an enormous risk in telling him anything more. But she didn't know what the risk truly was. She feared her father, yes, but was there another reason? She didn't know. She flashed to the nightmares. She'd had two more since moving in with Lowell. Blood. Thorns. Running. The red suitcase. Now, a phone. That had become the focus of the nightmares now. She wondered if it was all connected. She could feel memories bubbling, lingering just beneath the surface. She looked down at her hands, rubbed at the bits of skin around her cuticles, trying to smooth them down so she wouldn't pick at them.

"I am not pushing you, Jelly. I'm just worried. That's all. You can tell me more when you're ready. And only if you want to." He placed his cup on the side table, stood up from the couch, and headed to the bathroom. She was glad for the space. She trusted Lowell, but something in her gut told her: not yet.

"Get off her!" Grace screamed. She was standing in the doorway to the kitchen, clinging to her Raggedy Ann doll. It was new, a present from Nanny, given to her the day before for her fifth birthday. She was clutching the doll as her father held her mother to the floor, his hand around her throat. Mummy was trapped and Daddy was fumbling with his belt.

"Go back to bed, Grace," her mother gasped. "Please baby, go back to bed."

Her father ignored her, his entire focus on her mother. Grace backed away from the door and ran to her parent's bedroom. To her left was her parent's closet. It was dark and away from the screaming. She nestled herself into the back corner, gripping her doll as if it were the only thing that could protect her. The screaming scared her.

Moments later, she felt something in her hand. A phone. She stared down at the numbers. She couldn't remember the number Mummy told her to dial when this happened again. She heard noises from the kitchen, but she couldn't remember the number. Panic filled her. Something banged outside the front door. It sounded like fireworks, like the ones they saw the week before. She crawled out of the closet and toward the bedroom door. She didn't want Daddy to hear her. Peering around the corner, there by the front door, was a red suitcase. One lock was unlatched on the case, and there was something red underneath. Something that looked wet and sticky. She reached for the suitcase, but the muffled screams were coming from the kitchen again. It frightened her, so she crawled back to the closet, back into the corner. She picked up the phone again. This time, it felt cold. Ice cold. She looked down again, and it was a different phone in her hand. But the number. She still couldn't remember the number...

Grace woke up drenched in sweat. She couldn't catch her breath. She looked around the room manically, trying to place where she was. A streetlight was shining into the room. She was at Lowell's.

But the nightmare? What was that? She had been young. Five. And the doll? She remembered that doll. There'd been a little heart sewn onto its chest. Nanny had given it to her for her birthday. And the suitcase was in the dream again. And the phone. But this time, there were two phones. The more she thought about it, the more she knew something about these dreams was true. She just didn't know what. Had her mother been planning on taking them away to live with Nanny?

'Come home to me, sweetness. You'll be safe here.'

Were they not safe from her father? Was he the evil in all of this? He told Grace that her mother died of cancer. Something wasn't right with that. The red suitcase was the one thing that was constant in the nightmares. Now, she remembered that suitcase vividly. It was real. It was sitting at the door the night her mother died.

16

GRACE DECIDED to go to the movie with Daniel. He offered to pick her up, making it feel even more like a date. But she didn't want anyone knowing where she lived. What if her father figured out who Daniel was, and followed him to the apartment? Was she being paranoid? Probably. Lowell reminded her again that it was time to move her life forward, whether she was going on a date or as friends. She pondered this awhile, then finally sent the text to Daniel late Friday night.

Looking forward to it, Daniel replied quickly.

Me too, she responded.

Grace admitted to Lowell she'd never been to a movie before, something he found quite shocking. But she decided not to share that with Daniel. She wanted to seem normal for once. The last thing she needed was to make it obvious how much of a social freak she was. She was never one to fit in, but she was starting to feel like a normal teenager. Now, she *did* fit in. People accepted her. She didn't know who she really was, but at least people accepted the version of herself she revealed to them.

After their conversation the night of the chemist, Lowell had given her a lot to think about. She was used to this life of hiding. But sharing it felt like she was exposing herself, piece by piece. The nightmares felt exposing too. They'd prompted her to dissect everything John had said to her over the years. Now, she began wondering how many lies she'd been told.

Daniel's knock on the door on Saturday night was right on time. Nevertheless, Lowell answered the door as a precaution, while Grace hid in the bedroom. It was a system they'd agreed upon, in case John found her. When she heard Daniel's voice at the door, Grace stepped into the room.

"Hi!" he said, looking happy to see her.

"Hello," she replied. She wasn't sure what to say to him. He looked the same. He was dressed in jeans, a blue striped button-down shirt tucked in, his boots the same worn out ones he'd worn to the café. But something was different. It threw her off kilter. Grace dug into her shredded cuticles. What was she doing?

"Please, come on in," said Lowell, gesturing Daniel into the small space. The place was already crowded with two, but with Daniel here, she felt like the confined space would suffocate her.

"Can I get you a drink? A coke? Wine? Water?" Lowell offered. Daniel accepted water with thanks. While Lowell went into the kitchen, she and Daniel stared at each other. It was strange seeing him outside of the café, strange to be going on a non-date together. Daniel smiled, and it was enough to undo her. Shit. She was making a mistake. Grace excused herself and escaped to the bathroom. With her back against the closed door, she could hear their muffled conversation.

What was she doing? She barely knew the guy. She'd been nervous all day. When she arrived home after work, she tried explaining her anxiety to Lowell, but she struggled to find the words. Paranoid questions spun through her head. What if he was a spy? What if he was part of the group chasing them? What if he was what they'd been running from? Was she putting herself in danger? If she'd expressed those thoughts to Lowell, he'd think she was crazy. So, she kept it on the safe side and talked about Daniel's interest in dating her, but it did little to relieve her anxiety.

She placed her hand on her chest, willing her heart to slow down. The fabric of the one nice shirt she owned, a blue cotton blouse, felt scratchy on her fingers. She had few clothes because of situations like this. In case she had to run. She could pack a bag quickly if she only had a few things. Should she run?

"Hey Grace? Are you nearly ready to go?" Lowell called to her. Nearly ready? God no. But she knew those words held meaning, too. She trusted Lowell. If he asked her that, he must believe Daniel was okay. She took a deep breath, checked herself in the mirror, fixed her hair over her scar and turned back toward the door.

"Sorry," she said, coming out from the bathroom. She picked up her jacket from the back of the couch.

"Good to go?" Daniel asked, looking concerned. "The

movie starts in an hour, but it's a half hour to get there so…"

"Yep. Ready," she looked to Lowell nervously. He saw the pleading look and came over to hug her goodbye.

"He's okay. But call me if you need me to come and get you, alright?" he whispered in her ear. She nodded, but he didn't understand why she was so nervous. Why had she let him assume it was dating nerves? But she knew it was because she wasn't ready to yet. Grace grabbed her phone and backpack and followed Daniel out the door.

"Don't you kids have too much fun! But be careful if you do," Lowell sang as they left the apartment. Grace turned and stared daggers at him.

"Ignore him. We're two friends going to a movie. That's it," said Daniel, as they made their way down the stairs. At the street, Daniel opened the passenger door and gave Grace a hand up into his truck.

"Normally I'd let a mate make his own way into the truck, but I know it's pretty high. I still need to get the step installed," Daniel said, then made his way around to the driver's seat.

"You asked me to pick the movie, so I hope I've picked a good one. My friend Claire suggested it and I trust her. I've known her since we were kids." He started the engine. She'd yet to say a word. When the truck didn't move, she looked over at him, puzzled.

"Before we go… Are you sure you want to do this?" he asked. His hands rested on the steering wheel. "It's just, you're really quiet and if you're not up for a movie, that's okay."

She knew she had to relax. She looked up at the apartment. Knowing Lowell was inside made her feel more secure. He was her safety net now. But Lowell was right. She needed to get on with her life. This was the first step. Plus, she wouldn't have to talk to Daniel too much, since they were seeing a movie.

"Yes, I'm okay," she whispered, turning back to him. "Sorry."

"No need to apologise. Only wanted to make sure before we go." He put the truck in gear, turned his indicator on, checked the mirrors, and pulled out into the street.

When they reached the parking lot near the theatre, Grace slid out of the truck before Daniel could come around to help her out. Dates held doors. Not friends.

"I'm paying, by the way," Daniel said to her, holding the door open when they reached the theatre. NO! She wanted to scream: This is NOT A DATE!

"God, I can see you fighting me without you even saying a word. I've been a starving student too, so I know what it's like. I'm just being a friend, that's all. I swear." He raised his hands in the air in surrender, like he was being held at gunpoint. She didn't like it. This was way too much like a date.

"Plus," he added, his voice quieting, "I want to celebrate that you're away from your dad. Lowell seems like a good guy. I'm just happy to know you're safe." She didn't know why, but his comment embarrassed her. She was so grateful to Lowell, but she didn't like people thinking she was incapable of saving herself.

"I can pay for myself, Daniel," she said and started pulling her wallet from her backpack.

"I know you can Grace, but please. Let me do this. I'm just one friend helping another out." She hesitated. Her funds may be low, but she was still capable.

"Please," he said. Looking into his intense blue eyes, she finally relented.

"Wow! That was a great movie!" gushed Grace. She emerged from the theatre transformed, as if she'd just left a magical garden that made the impossible possible. She'd watched television before, but seeing a movie played out on such a vast screen was incredible. Not to mention the sweeping music that vibrated through her entire body! It was mind blowing. She'd been entranced as soon as the lights went down. She felt giddy with the rush of excitement.

When they opened the theatre door to the street, the place buzzed with traffic.

"I'm relieved you liked it. Claire said it was based on an actual story," he said. They stood to the side, just outside the theatre, trying to avoid the mass of people walking toward them.

"That scene though, with the toenail? Ugh, that was gross," she said. "They should warn you not to eat before watching that movie."

"Yeah, I've got an iron stomach, but even that was a bit much for me." Daniel paused a beat. "Okay. Next up, do you like hot chocolate?"

"Yes?" she responded, hesitantly. She didn't want to admit they'd been dinner occasionally, filling her up more than coffee ever could.

"Then let's go this way," Daniel said with a smile, and he pointed to the left toward the rail overpass. She felt more relaxed with Daniel after the movie, although she remained uncomfortable with the fact he'd paid. He not only bought the movie tickets but insisted on popcorn and drinks. She'd pay him back, she promised herself. This was not a date.

"I really liked that movie theatre. It was old and ornate and, I don't know, had character," she said, commenting on the Odeon Theatre they'd just left. She knew she was rambling. She was still buzzed from the movie.

"Yeah, it reminds me a bit of the one at home," said Daniel. He described the old-time theatre, explaining it was in the Southern Highlands, a few hours south of Sydney.

"And it's still running?"

"Yep. Every Tuesday, Friday, and Saturday nights, with matinees on Saturday and Sunday afternoons. It's never packed, unless it's the new release of a blockbuster, but it's never empty either. That's always a concern in a country town. Luckily, that's not the case with our movie theatre. This one's the same. I've been here a few times. It's always busy, which is great, given there's a large movie complex just down the road. Seems other people appreciate the charm of the old-time theatre too."

They walked down the ramp of the bridge, and he pointed ahead to the café.

"I'm glad you liked the movie. Claire has great taste in films. I liked the main character. She was strong. She reminded me of you," he said.

"She did?" The main character resonated with her.

Although she'd camped before, going on a three-thousand-mile hike was not something she'd ever imagined doing. She didn't know the conversion of miles to kilometres, but she knew it was an insane distance to walk.

"I wonder what it would be like. Hiking the PCT, I mean. It's a long way. I don't know if I could hack it."

"Really? I think you could. Have you been camping before?"

"Yeah," she said, non-committedly.

"We should go camping," he said. "Invite Lowell. Bring my friend Claire too. Maybe a few others." She tried to hide her snicker but was unsuccessful.

"What's funny?" asked Daniel.

"I don't see Lowell as one for camping. Camping for him would mean a five-star hotel in the city. But I'd go camping with you and your friends. Or, even with you on our own." Stunned, he looked at her. She blushed. What the hell was that? Camping? Alone with Daniel? She was fricking losing it.

"Well, we can talk about that idea later," he said, and opened the café door for her.

"Go grab a seat. I'll go and order our drinks," he said, and she started unzipping her backpack again. "Pay me back later. Go. The place is too busy to haggle right now." She looked around and didn't see an empty table in sight. He was right. It was busy.

A few minutes later, she grabbed a table by the window, just as two other people were leaving. She looked at Daniel standing in line. He'd behaved like a perfect gentleman all night. But she knew in her gut that it was a date. She just wasn't willing to admit that to Daniel yet.

Now that she had relaxed around him, she imagined that the date was going well. Not that she had any dating experience to draw from. She looked around. The place was filled with couples huddled together in intimate conversation. Others, girlfriends mostly, held hot drinks or shared sundaes between them. The place was noisy, but not boisterous. The street outside was empty but for people leaving the theatre, or a few walking to the train station. Yeah, this was definitely a 'date' kind of destination.

"Here you go," Daniel said, a little while later, placing two steaming white mugs on their wooden table. "I'm warning you though, there's no going back to regular hot chocolates after this."

"Yum, smells great," she admitted. The aroma made her mouth water. Two marshmallows sat beside the mug. She popped hers into her mug and watched them melt into the dark liquid.

"Between you and Lowell, I'm going to have to find a gym soon."

"Yeah, I don't think you need to worry. You only drink coffee from what I've seen."

"God, not you, too? Lowell's already on my case about my coffee habit."

"Just looking out for you. Probably the first time someone has in a while, I would bet. Besides Lowell I mean."

"Don't ruin this date by reminding me," she said. Her hand flew to her mouth as soon as the words left her lips. Her cheeks flamed crimson. But it was too late.

"A date, you say?" he asked quickly, picking up on her

slip. He picked up one of his marshmallows and popped it into his mouth. His blue eyes flared, never leaving hers.

"Let's just call it what it is," she said. She may have had a rough start tonight, but she was enjoying getting to know him. Her anxiety lessened, but she still felt a nervous energy being with him. "But I want to be clear. I have a clear goal. I need to stay focused on my H.S.C. It's too important," she said, looking at him intently.

"Then a date it is," he said and reached out for her hand. She let him take it. "And yes, I know you're focused on school. I respect that."

"One date won't kill me. Besides, you're probably a pro at this. You've probably been on a thousand dates by now."

"Not as many as you may think." She doubted that. He was too good looking. She certainly wasn't about to tell him this was her first. She took her hand back to pick up her mug. Slowly, she took a sip, feeling his eyes watching for her reaction, and she tried to stifle a groan. Wow, it was incredible, like heaven in a cup. Froth from the marshmallow lingered on her upper lip. He leaned over and brushed it off with his thumb before she realised it was there. Her stomach flipped, and she looked to her lap, embarrassed.

"Sorry," he said, reaching for her hand again.

"It's okay. It's me. This is so good. Like, amazingly good." He grinned, pleased with himself, and her stomach back flipped again. Yeah, this most definitely was a date. Shit.

17

Grace stopped abruptly in the doorway when she came home from work. Removing her key, she saw Lowell dash into his bedroom. She closed the door, then walking slowly into the apartment, peered into the bedroom. She found Lowell packing a small suitcase with urgency. Clothes covered the bed. Shoes were scattered on the floor below the suitcase. He seemed manic.

"What's going on? Are you okay?" she asked, setting her backpack down on the couch. Lowell's laptop lay open nearby. She noticed an email open on the screen but dared not read it.

"I have to go home," he snapped and threw a pair of jeans into the suitcase.

"What happened?" she asked, moving to the bedroom.

"Fucking Dad happened. I have to drive up there tonight." She quickly got out of his way as he dashed into the bathroom. "I'll be away for a few days. You'll be okay, yeah?"

"I'll be fine. Do… Do you want me to come with you?" she asked, listening to him rifle through drawers. From the look of the room, the drawers had to be empty by now. The place looked like an explosion of clothes.

"I mean, I can't drive," even though she knew she could, just not legally, "but I can be there for you. Help with whatever." It probably wasn't the best idea for her to go. There wasn't much she could do to help. She'd probably just be in the way, but she wanted to help Lowell with this. Whatever this was… He'd always been there for her. She nervously picked at her cuticles as Lowell returned to rummage through his bedroom closet.

"God Jelly, that would be great, but I don't want to put you in that scene again." Yeah, she didn't want to be in that scene either. She knew his dad was violent, and Lowell hadn't been home since his father nearly killed him. He had to have good reason to return.

"It's not like I don't know what it's like. Let me help. I can at least keep you awake while you drive." It was already nine o'clock on Friday night and she knew his parents lived nearly six hours away on the North Coast.

"Don't you have to work?" he asked, pausing on his packing.

"Nope, not scheduled until Monday afternoon, and if we're not back by then, I'll call in. And school is still out for another week, remember? I can study while you see your mum."

"Then yes, that would be great if you're up for it. I'm sure adrenaline will keep me awake for a bit, but a distraction from this shit show would be welcomed." She nodded, then dashed over to the bed and pulled her duffle from under the bed. Most of her stuff was still in it. She tossed in her jeans from the chair in the corner.

"Just need to grab my toothbrush and I'm ready to go."

"What? How? I've been packing for thirty minutes," he said. She wanted to answer 'experience' but didn't want to explain that now. But it was habit. She never knew when she would have to flee.

"Wait, don't you have a date tomorrow?" he said.

"Yes, but I'll text Daniel and tell him something came up. He'll understand." While she waited for Lowell, she pulled out her phone. Three weeks had passed since her first 'date' with Daniel. They were taking it slow and been out only a few times since. He was keeping to his word, respecting her schedule.

Something came up. Helping Lowell this weekend. Need to cancel tomorrow. Sorry. Talk soon. She hesitated, then added: *x.*

"He's solid. I'd do him," Lowell said, rushing back to the bathroom, as she finished up the text. Grace laughed. She knew Daniel was a good distraction from Lowell's situation.

"Yeah, except he doesn't play for your team. We've gone over this," she said and waited for him by the front door. She could hear Lowell zipping his toiletry bag, then his suitcase, and when the suitcase finally hit the floor, she picked up her duffel. Lowell walked to his laptop on the couch, hit the send button, closed the lid, and tucked it under his arm.

"Well, if Daniel ever realises he's gay, you will let me know, right?" he said, opening the front door. "Do you have everything? I can't believe you got ready that fast."

She nodded, waited until he locked the door, then lead the way down the stairs to the parking garage.

"So, what happened?" Grace asked once they got on the highway. Lowell, in his own head, looked to her with a confused look. "With your mum. You didn't say."

"Oh, she's in the hospital. Apparently, she was going to sneak down to see me. Dad was scheduled to be away on business, but the trip got cancelled. He came home to find her packed bag. Anyway, I got the call from the hospital. She had a card tucked into her handbag, listing me as her emergency contact. Not sure where Dad is."

"He's a politician, right?" Lowell nodded.

"We usually schedule our visits while he's working in Canberra. But for some reason he's locked down in his local office. Has been for weeks now. No clue why." The idea of his dad being around made her flinch. She wiped her sweaty palms along her pants. If the public learned of his violent tendencies, there'd be reporters, or even television. Maybe cops, too. Shit. She didn't think about that. She ran from cops. Not toward them.

Blend in. Those words haunted her.

"Is your mum alright?" she asked.

"Don't know. She was going into surgery when we left. Internal bleeding, they said. They told me she wouldn't say who did it. The neighbour found her lying in the garage, next to her car. The door was wide open."

"Oh God." She knew it had been the right choice to come with Lowell. He'd need the support. She'd deal with the rest. "She'll be okay, Lowell. I know it. If she's anything like you, she'll get through this."

They were silent for the next hour, once Lowell put on some upbeat music. Grace thought of her own father. She'd been looking over her shoulder for weeks. But now she had people around her. How she'd managed that after all these years, she didn't know, but she was relieved to have them. She'd even informed Miss O'Donnell about moving in with Lowell. She almost laughed when she saw the relief on her teacher's face. Her mind drifted back to Lowell's mother.

"Does your Mum have anyone else she can ask for help?" Grace asked. She knew she was asking a question she probably knew the answer to. Asking for help was hard. Sometimes impossible. And if Lowell's Dad was in the public eye, it would seem impossible to his mother.

"Don't know. She's never mentioned anyone else."

"Oh fuck," Lowell said through the dark minutes later.

"What?" He fumbled in his jacket pocket. "What are you looking for?" She felt a thump when something landed on her lap. His phone.

"I just realised, we can't stay at my parent's house, and I didn't find a place to stay. Can you look? Go to, like, booking.com or something. Find something near the hospital." He lifted in his seat, found his wallet, and tossed that to her too. "My credit card is in there."

"Sure," she said. For the next twenty minutes, she looked for a place to stay.

"How many nights do you want? Two? Three?" she

asked once she found three motels that were budget friendly and a short distance to the hospital.

"Just book two nights. We can always add on if we need to. Make sure they know it's a late check in tonight. We'll hit the hospital first, then get sleep." She doubted sleep was happening tonight, but figured Lowell would need a bed early tomorrow, once he knew what was going on with his mother. Grace hadn't thought of a hotel. She assumed they'd be sleeping in the car. She'd done that plenty of times before.

The dawn light filtered softly into the hospital room. Grace looked over at Lowell, asleep in the chair beside his mother's bed. He looked like a rumpled mess, so unlike his perfectly tidy self. But he was exhausted. It had been an insanely long night.

Grace sat on the floor on the opposite side of the room, her back against the wall. She let her mind wander. She was furious with herself. She could have driven at least part of the way. Lowell would be in better shape to help his mum if she did. She knew how to drive, she'd learned at twelve through necessity. Her Dad would have killed them both long ago otherwise.

She was also angry for Lowell and for his mother. His mother now lay between them, a tiny, broken woman, lost amongst the bedsheets. Her face looked ashen, and she had all kinds of tubes connected to her. She had been wheeled in from surgery a few hours before. The damage was extensive, they'd said, but she would survive. He was asked if he knew who would do this to his mother and as he stood beside her, holding her hand, tears streaming down his face, he told them he didn't know. But he knew. Grace could see it on his face.

Now, the room was quiet but for the hospital machinery buzzing and beeping around them. Grace stood, stretched, and left the room. She needed coffee. For most, it provided a jolt of caffeine. For her, it was comfort. This pain was too close to home.

From out of nowhere, she thought of red walls, a red suitcase, and a phone. Jesus, where had that come from? Her nightmares were still present, but she'd not had one in the last week. At Lowell's, she could finally sleep through the night. But the nightmares were still on her mind since they began eight months ago.

She followed the hallway back toward reception. The cafeteria was on the other side of the hospital. When Grace turned the corner, she froze. An older man, dressed in a dark grey suit, stood at the counter screaming at the receptionist. His face was dark, both in colour and intent, and she knew instantly it was Lowell's father.

"Where the hell is my wife? I want to see her. Now!" His baritone voice boomed through the halls. Grace looked behind her, back toward Lowell's mother's room, relieved to see the empty corridor.

"What is wrong with you? My wife. Nellie Kanu. Where is she?" The voice was laced with something she knew all too well. But he wasn't slurring his words. No, this was undiluted rage.

Grace turned on her heel and ran back to the room, away from the monster. She needed to warn Lowell.

1 8

"LOWELL, WAKE UP," Grace hissed, rocking his arm gently, then looking toward the door in a panic. She looked back, shook harder. Lowell's eyes opened, focused on her.

"Your father is here. In reception. He was screaming at the woman behind the desk." Lowell snapped wide awake. He rubbed his eyes and saw his mother coming awake now. She must have heard her too. She looked worriedly at Lowell.

"Don't worry Mumma, I've got this." He stood straight, pulled his wrinkled shirt down, kissed his mother's forehead and walked toward the door. There, he met his father.

"What the hell are you doing here?" his father snapped, trying to push him aside, but Lowell held up his hand, blocking his entry, and stared at his father. Grace, standing by his mother's bed, quietly reached over and took Nellie's shaking hand.

"I said, what are you doing here? You are not welcome here," his father roared. The nurses at the desk looked up at the disturbance, one picking up the phone discreetly.

"I'd say the opposite is true, Father. You're the one not welcome here," said Lowell, his voice steady.

"Oh, you can go to hell, boy. Who do you think you are, telling me where I can be? She is my wife!"

"Men do not beat the women they love. They protect them."

"Well, you're not a man. We've already established that fact," his father's voice hissed at him, his eyes boring into Lowell's. He tried again to get past, but Lowell held his ground. There was movement by the elevators.

"I do not wish to see my husband," Nellie said, her voice barely a whisper, but it was loud enough for all to hear her message.

"I have a right to be here," his father bellowed, then looked directly at Lowell and added, "She's mine."

Something about that sentence made the hairs on Grace's neck stand up. She looked to Nellie. Tears shone in the woman's eyes. Defeat reflected in them. Grace untangled their hands and walked toward Lowell, standing behind him.

"Who the hell are you?" Lowell's father shifted his attention to Grace.

"It doesn't matter who I am. But these two people? They are not possessions. Not something you own. They are people. Loving people. Caring people. People who deserve love and understanding. And they deserve respect. Your son is an amazing person, an amazing son, and an amazing friend. You are an idiot for throwing him out. But maybe that's best because he's a much better man than you appear to be. Nellie has expressed she doesn't want you here, so you need to leave. Now."

She didn't know where the words came from, but she meant every single syllable. She stood taller behind Lowell. His father's anger intensified. She expected a fist, a backhand, something, but the nurse and two security guards walking toward them got his attention.

"Sir? You need to leave. You are not on the approval list for this patient," the nurse said, brandishing her clipboard like a weapon.

"Like hell I'm not. I'm her husband, for God's sake."

"Sir, you need to leave," the security guards moved closer. Lowell's chin jutted out defiantly. Grace stared the man down.

"Then you can take the useless woman home with you. She's not welcome in my house. Especially if she supports the likes of you. You can all rot in hell."

And with that, Lowell's father turned and stormed past the security guards, but they followed him down the hall.

Nellie broke out in tears and Grace stepped aside to let Lowell go to her.

"I'm sorry Mumma. I thought it was the best thing," said Lowell, taking her hand, kissing it. Grace bowed her head, trying to disappear from the scene.

"Come here, my girl," the woman whispered. Nellie and Lowell were looking right at her. Their faces held the same look, but she couldn't read its meaning. She screwed up. Shit. She felt the sting of salty tears on her lashes. Had she made things worse? What sparked her to speak up?

"I'm so sorry. I am so, so sorry. I didn't mean…" Lowell stepped toward her and pulled her into a hug.

"Thank you Jelly. Not only for coming with me, but for that, what you did there. You are a brave woman, braver than I ever believed. Thank you for sticking up for us. For being on our side."

"Well, sure. I mean, you've been there for me and…. But I hope…"

"Stop there," he said, and led her back to his mother's bed. The woman opened her hand again and Grace took it. The woman squeezed her fingers.

"Zaki. Call Aunty Sharn. She'll know what to do."

"Aunty Sharn?" he asked, surprised. His mother nodded. He looked to Grace.

"She is my mother's oldest friend. We moved to Queensland when we first moved to Australia to be near her. She and my mother grew up together in Nigeria, before my mother moved to England. I think I was about ten when we moved south for my father's job." He glanced back at his mother.

"You stayed in touch?" His mother nodded. "Then Mumma, why didn't you call her before this?" His mother simply shook her head, but Grace understood why she stayed silent.

Staying was too hard to explain.

With his mother's phone in hand, Lowell left the room to call his aunt.

"Why do you call him Zaki?" Grace asked. It was a strange nickname. There had to be a story behind it.

"It means sweetness in Hausa, my mother's Nigerian language," she explained. "He's been sweet since the day he was born." Nellie smiled at Lowell, standing outside the door, his face now in a broad smile.

"You know how Lowell always likes to call people funny pet names? Well, he got that from me. Now, child. Tell me the story of why he calls you Jelly." Grace looked to Lowell and smiled, then told his mother about her own nickname, the one she'd finally come to accept with affection.

"You know Zaki, I was just thinking of the last time we were in this hospital together," Nellie said when Lowell returned.

"That was a long time ago now," he said, looking pained, handing her back her phone.

"You looked broken in this hospital bed," she continued, her eyes finding his. She glanced at Grace, as if to ask a question.

"It's okay Mumma, she knows what happened."

"I thought you were dead when I walked into this room," she said. "You had everything wrapped in bandages. Your right leg, in that cast, and elevated. And your face? Sweet Jesus. You were unrecognisable. But I knew it was more than that. Deeper than that."

"I almost died Mumma. He didn't hold back. But it wasn't his fists that nearly killed me. His hatred broke me. It took me a long time to get past his awful words. I only wish he didn't take that out on you." Lowell said, his voice carrying the guilt he so clearly felt. "I actually believed, coming out to you both, that it would free me. But it did the opposite. I felt more trapped by what he said to me than before. Took me a long time to realise his words weren't my truth."

"I know you were in hospital for a long time," his mother said. "I know it was more than just broken bones that kept you here. Then I heard..." Her voice cracked. "I heard you tried to kill yourself after that."

Grace looked down at the semi-colon tattoo on Lowell's wrist.

"You should have filed charges, Zaki. Your father was expecting the police to show up at the door every day. For weeks." Lowell looked at his mother with tears in his eyes. When he'd explained that time to Grace, he told her he could've ended his life, but he chose not to because of his mother. Grace was thankful for that for so many reasons.

"I couldn't press charges, Mumma. Not while you were still there. And I knew he had connections. Neither of us would be safe if I did," Lowell said, squeezing his mother's hand. "It was hard enough getting letters from you and not being able to reply. I'm just grateful for our lunches. I'm sorry he found out about them."

"Well, that's in the past now. Sharn and Jerome have a nice little granny flat out the back of their house. Sharn has been trying to get me to move in there for years," Nellie said. Lowell looked surprised. "Oh, she knows everything. And don't worry, I'll be safe there. Jerome has also been hinting he has his own connections. I haven't mentioned them to your father in over twenty years. He'll never suspect I'm with them."

As Grace listened to their conversation, she recalled

when Lowell first told her about the lunch rendezvous with his mother. They each drove four hours, every other month, just to have lunch together. Grace didn't know how he did it with his busy life, but it never fazed him. The bond they shared was too important to them both to worry about such things. She wondered what her own mother would have done to protect her.

Two nights later, with Sharn and Jerome heading north with Nellie, Lowell and Grace headed south toward home. Lowell was relieved to know his mother was in excellent hands. By the time his mother's oldest friends arrived, Sharn had arranged everything. The doctors would release Nellie to the hospital six hours north, under Sharn's care. Sharn, a retired ICU nurse, assured Lowell that privacy laws would not allow either hospital to disclose anything to Lowell's father. The transfer was seamless.

"I think we need some tunes, Jelly. Your choice. Just no hip hop," said Lowell, his tone much lighter. "I just need something to keep us driving until Sydney."

"You know, I can drive if you need me to. I mean, I don't have my license, but I know how to drive."

"Why don't you have your license then?" He looked over at her, the oncoming headlights highlighting their faces.

"I don't know…" she responded and realised there was no reason for her not to have her license now. Before, her father said it was so they couldn't be tracked. But now she felt that whoever was after them, they were after her father. Not her.

"Lack of funds, I imagine," he suggested. She nodded, letting him think it was financial. What would be involved in getting her license? Would she need identification? Surely, they needed something. That was a problem. She only had fake papers.

A POUNDING CAME at their door. Grace almost dropped the bowl she was drying. Lowell looked at her, suds covering his hands in the sink. Shaking her head, she quietly placed the bowl on the counter.

"Are you expecting Daniel tonight?" he asked quietly. She shook her head. "I'm not expecting anyone either." He wiped his hands and walked to the door. He peered through the peephole and pulled back fast, turning to her.

"Police?" he mouthed. Grace felt the wind go out of her lungs. On instinct, she threw down the tea towel and rushed into the bathroom to hide behind the door. Lowell opened the front door.

"Good evening. Sorry to bother you. We're looking for a Grace, ah," the officer paused, "Thompson. Does she live here?"

"No, but we're friends." Grace was relieved to hear Lowell was savvy enough to lie about where she lived. She was grateful for his protection.

"May we come in?" he asked. "We have a few questions."

Then silence. Shit.

Grace heard footsteps on the wood floor. Two sets. One wearing police-commissioned boots and the other wearing… heels? The door closed behind them. Her heart raced. Why were they looking for her? People only came looking for her father. Had something happened to him? Or had Miss O'Donnell called the police after all?

"Is Miss Thompson here with you? We have some questions pertaining to her father," the policewoman asked.

"No, not tonight. Is there something I can help you with?"

"Are you Mr. Kanu? You're the one on the lease here?"

"That's right." Grace hated herself for putting Lowell in this situation. Especially after everything he'd been through over the last week. And how did they even find her?

"Grace's father, Mr. Thompson, has been arrested. Her name came up in our conversation with him. He said his daughter had, ah, 'flown the coop'. To be honest, it's taken us a while to find her, but we have some questions we need to ask her. We finally tracked her down through school records. She, um, lists this place as her address?" They were being vague. But what was her father arrested for? It had to be drug related. It was surprising he hadn't been caught already. "If you can ask Grace to call me. We'd like very much to speak with her."

"Of course. I'll let her know." When the door closed

after the officers left, Grace let out her breath. Now she had to face Lowell.

She tiptoed out of the bathroom and peeked around the corner toward the front door. Lowell watched through the peephole. She jumped when he turned around quickly.

"Want to take five guesses what that was about?"

"I heard."

"He's been arrested. You're safe." For tonight, she thought. Her father would wonder if she was the one that called the police. He'd accused her of doing that in the past. They'd evaded the police many times before. It would spark his need to find her. She looked at her cuticles, picked at some skin edging up. The shame she felt was unbearable. She couldn't look at Lowell.

"You need to call them. They left a card. They'll be back if you don't." She nodded, working her ravaged fingers. How could she avoid them? What questions could they have for her? Did she need to run? She didn't want to. She'd found safety here. Life was good. A trickle of warm blood blossomed, giving her a moment of comfort.

"I'll call them tomorrow morning." She worried the police would still be outside, waiting for her. She had to work out what to do before morning. Normally it was her father deciding what to do, when to run, but now it was all on her.

"Jelly." She looked up at Lowell. "I'm right here. I can protect you." She doubted that, but it was nice to hear he was willing.

"You were brave with my dad. I know you have it in you. Now, you need to stand up to John, just as you did with my father," he said, then returned to the dishes. If only it were that simple.

Grace was wide awake before the sun came up the following morning. She tried not to move until she knew Lowell was awake in the lounge room. No matter how quiet they tried to be, once one was up, so was the other. There was no room for privacy in the tiny space.

"Lowell," she whispered into the morning light.

"Yeah, Jelly?" he responded. His voice sounded deep and croaky, like he got as little sleep as she did.

"I'm going to call them this morning. I need to know if he's going to come after me."

"Why? Wait, I need the loo." He threw his bed covers back and padded to the bathroom in his boxer briefs and an AC/DC t-shirt.

When the bathroom door closed, Grace got up, dressed, made her bed quickly, then walked into the kitchen to put the kettle on. It was almost boiling by the time Lowell emerged, looking a lot more awake than he'd sounded minutes before.

"Cups are ready… just need water. My turn," she said, then walked to the bathroom. She felt guilty leaving Lowell to deal with the police the night before. No, she wouldn't bring him any further into it.

Lowell handed her a steaming cup of coffee when she returned.

"So, you're calling them? Want me to stay with you?" She nodded.

"I'm sorry to have done that to you last night. Me, hiding, I mean. That wasn't fair."

"I get it. Who knows what the manipulative bastards in our lives would do?" Grace looked at him with gratitude and took a sip of her coffee. Maybe he understood? At least some of it.

"I'm your friend, Jelly. Friends help each other, remember?" Lowell walked over to the table where they kept their keys and bags. He retrieved the officer's card and handed it to her. She read the card.

"This… the policewoman is a detective. From Victoria." Her voice was faint.

"Yeah, I noticed that too," he said, sipping his coffee. "Seems odd, don't you think?"

Whatever it was, she needed to understand what her father was doing and what he had dragged her into.

"Hello, I'd like to speak to Detective, um, O'Neal, please? Oh… my name is, um, Grace Thompson. She came to my friend's apartment last night and said she needed to ask some questions about my father?" She paused. "His name? John Thompson. Yes, that's right. Her card says Victoria Police, but this number was handwritten on the back of the card. Yes, I'll hold." Her hand was shaking. Lowell sat on the floor watching her. She tried to smile at him, but she knew it came out like a grimace.

"Oh! Yes, hello. I am. He has? May I ask what for? Okay. Ah, no, not that I'm aware of. Yes, yes, that's fine. I'll be at Lowell's. Yes, thank you. Bye."

She sat back against the couch, tossing the phone aside like it was a scorching hot potato.

"They'll be here in twenty minutes. Guess I'm going to be late for school again."

"Call that teacher who helped you," suggested Lowell. "Let her know the situation. Maybe she'll cover for you. I'll drop you off at school afterwards. My classes don't start until one and I was going to study until then. Did they say how long it'll take? The questions they want to ask?"

"No. They didn't. I'm so sorry, Lowell." He waved her off.

Grace sat on the couch with a pillow in her lap, her feet tucked under her. The detective sat next to her and opened her notepad. The woman, about fifty, wore a no-nonsense dark grey suit with a very stark white shirt. Very detective-like, if television was anything to go on. The detective came alone this time, a relief to Grace. She hated the police. Just seeing someone in uniform made her nervous. But just because she didn't wear the uniform didn't mean the detective could be trusted.

Lowell excused himself and retreated to the kitchen to make more coffee. He knew her too well. She could use another cup, maybe another five, just to get through this.

"So, Grace, let's start with what I know. Is that okay?" Grace nodded. The woman smiled at her. Grace couldn't tell if it was genuine. Probably not, just practiced. Grace stiffened.

"Your father was arrested two nights ago on possession charges, aggravated assault and attempted robbery."

The only thing in that sentence that surprised Grace was the attempted piece. He must have been high if he couldn't pull off the robbery.

"Where?" Grace asked, her voice barely loud enough for her own ears.

"Pardon?" the detective looked up at her in confusion.

"Where was he arrested? Your business card… it said Victoria Police."

"Oh. He was arrested here, in the western suburbs. Penrith, I think," said the detective, referring to her notes.

"Then why are you asking me questions?" The question was double-barrelled. She wasn't connected to her father anymore. She made sure not to leave a trace of him, so how had they found her? And why were the Victoria police questioning her if he was arrested in Sydney? It made little sense.

"Well, that's why I'm here to talk to you. I have a friend in the district where he was arrested. She knows I've been working on a cold case from about twelve years ago, down in Melbourne. When your father was arrested, they found no record for him. My friend found that interesting, especially when she noticed his rather distinctive tattoo, one that fit with the profile of the missing man in the case I'm working."

Grace knew exactly what tattoo she was talking about. The detective was right. The black crow on his shoulder was very distinctive. When Grace remained silent, the detective continued.

"The cold case I'm working on involves a man and his daughter who went missing twelve years ago." Okay, she had her attention now. "No one has seen or heard from them since. At first, it was believed they were murdered. The mother is dead. That we know for sure. The man I'm looking for has a long police record, and he did not go by the name of John Thompson. Fake IDs are not hard to come by for the man I'm looking for. The little girl's name was Grace. These details seem a little too coincidental, so I came to Sydney to follow up on what my friend found."

Lowell came in and handed coffees to Grace and to the detective. Grace knew he heard every word. The kitchen wasn't that far away.

"Do you know anything about this Grace?" the detective asked, then thanked Lowell for the coffee.

"No, I don't. My father has never been to jail before. I mean, he's not perfect, but he's not a criminal." Lowell coughed, then Grace saw him reposition himself awkwardly out of the corner of her eye. It was enough to catch the detective's attention. Grace uncrossed her legs and put the pillow to the floor. It was time to move the detective on.

"And you don't think it's odd they have the same tattoo?" The detective placed her coffee on the side table.

"Well, yes. I do. But maybe it was done at the same tattoo place? Maybe they had a picture of it and thought it looked cool? I don't know…"

"There were a few other odd things about the disappearance. We found a red suitcase by the front door of the house, like someone was planning to leave. We also found a mobile phone in the woman's closet. Numbers had been punched in, but no calls were made."

Grace went cold. Exactly like her nightmare. She remained silent. But this time, she couldn't speak if she tried. Everything was a little too real. And she still didn't know who, or what, they were running from. But the suitcase. The phone. Her mother…

"Well, it would be nice to get some answers before I head back to Melbourne. Your father will be released on bail in the next few days if no other evidence turns up. Considering he doesn't have a record, that is."

2 0

For the next hour, Grace paced the apartment. Should she run? Her father was locked up. But for how long? She didn't want to change her address to Lowell's, but the school was making sure everyone's address was correct for the H.S.C. exam requirements. Ugh. If the detectives found her, her father would too, once he got out.

But the detective knew, just as she did, they couldn't hold her father without Grace's help. What had her father done? Something wasn't right. She never asked what he'd been arrested for, not really. The detective's answer was kind of vague. Probably on purpose. Should she have asked about the tattoo the detective referenced? Her silence probably gave the impression she knew about it. Shit. Of course she knew. As the detective said, it was distinctive. Did it mean something else? Why would the detective know about it?

Grace bit her fingernails, stripping the nail from the bed like she was stripping corn from the cob. If she ran, where would she go? Did she need to run? Who, or what, would she be running from? Her father told her they were running from 'bad people'. Probably more bullshit. She didn't know who to trust anymore. Maybe Lowell was in on it? Or Daniel? Maybe one of them was part of whatever it was her father was caught up in? Snitches worked for the police. Maybe that's how they found him? No. God, no. What was she was thinking? She was being stupid. Paranoid.

"Grace?" Lowell's voice startled her out of her panic. She was shaking all over. The part that made things real for her were the suitcase and the phone. It was too much like her dream.

"Come on, sit. I'll make you breakfast." She shook her head. "You need to eat."

No time. She needed to…

"Grace…" Lowell came toward her. She backed up, suddenly fearful of everyone, everything.

"Geezus. What did she say that has you so scared?" She shook her head. She zipped around him and walked into the bedroom, got into the bed, and pulled the covers up around her. Lowell followed her into the room and sat on the other side.

"Jelly, talk to me. I'm on your side, remember?" She shook her head. But her gut told her he was right. He'd always been there. But after the years of running, of always looking over their shoulder, she just didn't know what was true. And the red suitcase and the phone the detective mentioned…

"Jelly…"

"The suitcase. The phone. I keep dreaming about them."

"From the cold case?" She nodded, tears building.

"Maybe you read about it somewhere? Maybe it stayed in your head?"

"No. It's the nightmares I keep having. Running. Thorns. Blood. Hiding. Moving. My dad. Sometimes I see my mum in them too. But the red suitcase has been in every nightmare over the last six months. Sometimes open on the bed. But lately, by the front door. One of the last ones had blood coming out of the suitcase. And the phone? That's recent. I keep dreaming of being in the back of a closet with a phone in my hand, not being able to remember what number my mum told me to dial." She was always young in that part of the nightmare, she realised. Very young. Like, five. Twelve years the detective said.

Lowell was quiet, and when she glanced at him, his face was pale with pure shock. He said nothing for a long while.

"I should have told you. I'm so sorry," she said, tears trickling silently down her cheeks.

"So, what are you saying? That what the detective says is true? You've been on the run with your dad all these years?"

"Yes," she confided, letting that sink in. Then she added the thing that was concerning her more. "But I don't know why."

. . .

Lowell headed to the kitchen. She heard sounds of the toaster, the kettle. Her mind was going a million miles an hour, like her memories were on a newsreel. They whizzed through, going from one moment to the next. She tried to piece things together, but it was all too confusing. She needed to slow things down. Lowell came back into the bedroom with two cups and a plate piled high with jam-smothered toast. He handed her the steaming hot mugs.

"It's tea. Not coffee. You don't need any more today." She smirked, said thanks. He was trying to wean her off the stuff. He sat down on the bed opposite her, setting the plate of hot toast between them, then reached over to take a cup from her.

"My mother's name was Zoe, but that's all I know," Grace said. "Dad never talked about her, except in fits of rage. But it's only been recently. I have no photos of her, only memories, and even those memories are kind of sketchy. Dad destroyed the photos of my mother in a drunken stupor one night. I think I was about six but it's one thing I vividly remember." The mug burned her fingers, so she placed it on the bedside table, avoiding Lowell's gaze. She grabbed a pillow from the other side of the bed and wrapped her arms around it.

"We were living out of the car. Camping, kind of. Dad sat there, staring into the fire, and then suddenly, he got up, went to the car, and pulled something from the wheel well. Then he sat there and, one by one, threw her photos on the fire. I tried to stop him, but he was too strong and he pushed me to the ground. I remember because it was muddy. The wet grass soaked through my pants while I sat there and watched the images of my mother burn in the fire. He muttered one word, over and over, so softly, like he was in a trance. Fence. Fence. I still think that's weird." Maybe, she realised now, he was saying evidence? She shook her head. No, that would be…

"I never understood the level of his hatred toward her. I remember him hitting her, the same as he hit me. But I only remember snippets of that time. But, when it was just me and her? We were happy." She could feel the tears well again and wiped them away.

"I think we were five or six when we began to move around. Mum wasn't with us. He told me she'd died of cancer when I finally asked a few years later. He was scary, so I never asked before that. I think we stayed in Melbourne awhile, but we moved into a different house every few months. Dad told me it was because he'd been fired, had quit, the job didn't fit. Most days, I didn't even go to school. I was looked after by someone, usually the wife of a friend, but I was always reading. Even then. I think I was about thirteen when he started hitting me. I guess I started to backtalk, you know, forming my own opinions?" She knew she was rambling now, but she had to get this out. She still avoided Lowell's eyes. He stayed silent, but she could hear him sipping his tea.

"One night, Dad announced we were leaving Melbourne. After that, we began looking over our shoulders, hiding more. Camping in the bush. I was sixteen, nearly seventeen, when we eventually moved into the apartment in North Ryde. He said it was easier to hide in a city, but you still had to blend in. I was just glad we'd stayed in one place by then. You know the rest from there."

She was quiet for a few minutes. She picked up her tea.

It was cool now. She took a big gulp and coughed when the liquid went down the wrong way. Lowell got her a glass of water.

"The thing I can't figure out… he told me he got in with a dangerous crowd. That's why we were running. He never said who was after us. But he was super nervous around police. I figured that was because of this group he was mixed up with."

"You told me about the campervan on the ferry. Do you think that was part of it?"

"I don't know. At the time, I believed it was a game. Or that he couldn't afford my ticket. But I have been thinking about it since I told you about it. Now I wonder if he was trying to hide me, so they wouldn't see a man and a daughter? I remember we didn't stop in Melbourne. We drove right through to the east coast. We didn't even stop for a bathroom, which I desperately needed after hiding all night. I ended up wetting my pants." She hated to admit that part. It was hard enough admitting her actual story to Lowell. But she trusted him. He wasn't part of whatever it was her father was caught up in. The look on his face when she told him about her nightmares confirmed that much.

"And your hair. The colour."

"Yeah, he told me it was too much like my mother when it was blonde, and it made him sad. Which makes little sense, given his anger toward her. But I've been wondering about that too. I wonder now if it's coloured because…" she didn't even want to finish that thought.

"You really would look fabulous as a blonde, you

know? Shorter hair and blonde. Killer look." Grace winced.

"Sorry. I guess the blood part of your nightmares is still a question. And why run?" She nodded. She didn't know why, and it was bothering her now. "Don't worry Jelly. We'll figure it out."

"Before or after the detective does? If she hasn't already figured it out by now."

"What was the tattoo she was talking about? You've never mentioned a tattoo before."

"It's a black crow on his shoulder." She tapped her left shoulder blade. "It's big. Ominous. The detective was right. The tattoo is definitely unique."

"What does it mean? Most people have a tattoo because they relate to it somehow or it holds some meaning." Grace glanced down at the semi-colon tattoo on his wrist and nodded.

"Dad told me, years ago, that he got it when he was young, because he loved crows. They were mysterious, he told me, just like we were."

"Do you think it means something else?"

"I don't know." Did it? She wondered about that.

"Okay, so what about the no criminal record thing?" Lowell crossed his legs on the bed. "I'm sorry for coughing right when she said that. It wasn't intentional. But I find it odd that he doesn't have a record, as violent as he is and into drugs as much as you say. That just doesn't fit. He would have a DUI or something at least."

"He's gotten a speeding ticket before. We were north of Brisbane. And I know he was arrested for a DUI when we lived down in Gippsland, in Victoria. But he was using a different name then."

"What is his name? What's yours? Is it Grace?"

"His name has always been John. I've always been Grace. My mother even called me that before she died, so I think that's real. I don't know what our last name is anymore."

"Do you know how your mother died? Do you remember?"

"Cancer. That's what my father said. It would explain why I remember always being at the hospital with her. I remember that much. But I was young when she died."

"Do you believe that? That it was cancer?" he pushed. She paused for quite a while, then shrugged.

"I don't know what to believe anymore," she sighed.

2 1

Detective O'Neal called the following morning and asked Grace if she'd remembered anything more. While Grace remembered a lot more, there was nothing she was willing to share with the detective. She didn't know why she was protecting her father now, but she knew there had to be a reason he took her with him when they ran. That was the piece she couldn't figure out.

She left for school, slinging her backpack easily over her shoulders. It had been a while since she'd felt this good physically. Emotionally, she was still a mess. Jumping on to the train, she smiled at the elderly woman sitting in the disabled seat and took the seat behind her. The latest news about her father kept her on edge. She watched for odd behaviour. Her instincts were strong, something she'd honed over the years. She knew someone was going to pick-pocket before it happened, sensed when an older man was about to hit on a young girl. She longed to stick her headphones in, gaze at her phone and shut the world out like other teens. But she'd never been given that luxury.

When Grace arrived at school, she walked straight into Miss O'Donnell's classroom.

"Good morning, Miss. Did you get my email yesterday?" she asked, whispering to the teacher at the front of the room as the classroom settled. Once she knew she wasn't going into school yesterday, she let the school know. Lowell's suggestion to reach out to the teacher was a good idea.

"I did, Grace. It's okay. It's an excused absence." Grace hadn't told the teacher why she was absent, just that something came up. She only hoped the detective hadn't come to her school too.

"Thank you, Miss," she said and turned to walk to her seat.

"Everything okay?" the teacher asked before she got too far. Grace turned, smiled.

"Yes. Fine. Thank you."

She spent the day mulling over the information the detective shared and comparing it with what she knew, trying to piece things together. She fluctuated between anxious and angry, distracted, and unfocused. Whatever her dad was mixed up in, it was his fault they were on the run. His fault she had this thing looming over her. His fault she was struggling to move on.

"Miss Thompson? Are you going to answer the question?" her Maths teacher asked. She looked up and felt the heat rush straight to her cheeks.

"Sorry, Sir. What was the question?" It had been like this most of the morning. Thankfully, the bell rang for lunch before the teacher could ask her the question again. She mumbled her apologies when she headed outside with the rest of the class.

I'm pissed. I am so angry at him. Grace texted Lowell, her fingers flying over the keys.

Your Dad? She was relieved when he responded quickly.

Yeah. I don't know what he's up to, but I'm done.

She paused before hitting send, then added: *Let's colour my hair.*

No response. Hmm. She waited for a few minutes. Well, fine. She'd colour it, whether Lowell helped her or not. His text came in five minutes later.

I may have a better solution. I'm pinning new fliers for the studio at the local community board. The Hairdressing School is looking for volunteers. Specifically, for brunettes wanting to go blonde.

Sign me up!

Wait. It's tonight.

Good. Better now than never.

Grace sat in the stylist's chair, picking at her cuticles. The room was insanely loud and there were way too many people in it for Grace's liking. A young apprentice stood behind her, painting dye through her hair with a brush. At least she assumed that's what was happening. It was far different from how she did it at home.

Lowell dropped her off on the way to his class, and right now, she was freaking out. She wished Lowell was there. He was a calming force. There were two 'briefs', as they called it, happening in the school tonight. Hair cutting and colouring. Now, with her hair eighteen centimetres shorter, she stared at her image and heard her father's words: *Blend in.* Chopping her hair off and going blonde was the total opposite of that.

And right now, the apprentice assigned to her looked very nervous. Grace noticed her hands shaking and she would not shut up.

"It's like, really hard to go from brunette to blonde," the girl said. Grace guessed she was about seventeen, but she looked twelve. Her hair was bleached to an unnatural white-blonde, with some weird teal colour threaded through. The orange eyeshadow was an interesting contrast to the look.

"Some people, well, their hair goes orange. And, like, it's really hard to get it normal from there." The girl was not helping Grace's anxiety at all.

"Maddii!" The Supervisor's high-pitched scorn reverberated across the room. How the supervisor heard the girl, Grace did not know, but she was relieved she had. The girl smiled meekly at her in the mirror. Maybe now Maddii would shut up and get on with it.

When the apprentice was done painting, she stuck her under a dryer, thrust a magazine at her and told her she'd be back. Grace left the magazine on her lap and closed her eyes, willing her anxiety to tamper down.

She heard a timer go off and her dryer being lifted, so she opened her eyes again. Maddii looked down at her, picked up her hair, unwrapped a foil, then put the dryer down, setting another five more minutes on the dryer. Hopefully, her hair wouldn't end up bleached like Maddii's. The supervisor assured her it would be a 'lovely honey blonde by the end of the evening', but she didn't see the supervisor anywhere on this inspection.

By the time Lowell returned, Grace was pale, and her cuticles were shredded.

"How's it going, Jelly?" He looked at her hair, plastered in purple goop.

"My hair turned orange. So now they're turning it purple. I don't know what they've done Lowell, but it's not good." Grace hadn't seen Maddii in a while. The supervisor had taken over.

"Don't worry, you won't walk out of here with purple hair. They have a reputation to uphold. I checked into them earlier today. You'll be okay Jelly."

"You will," said the older supervisor, approaching them from behind. "I'll make sure of it. You said your hair had been dyed for a while?" Grace nodded, fear and concern stealing her voice.

"Don't worry. You will leave here in less than an hour looking fabulous, I promise." And with that, the woman walked away to inspect another apprentice's work. Maddii had been side-lined, but Grace knew it was not her fault. Grace hadn't been completely honest about how long her brunette colour had been in. Maybe that affected the outcome after all.

"I'm going to head over to Woolies. Don't worry, I'll be back in an hour to get you. It'll be great, Jelly."

• • •

An hour later, Grace gazed at her image in the mirror. She couldn't believe what she saw. Her hair had been cut into a chin-length bob. Her naturally curly hair had been cut by the supervisor in such a way it fell into 'beach waves', the apprentices gushing over it. It was slightly shorter at the back, and, feeling it with her hand, Grace decided she liked it. It was modern and it felt so soft. She'd never had her hair professionally cut before.

"Wow, she was right! You do look fabulous, Jelly. That colour is amazing!" Lowell exclaimed, walking back in with bags in his hands. Grace leaned into the mirror, studied herself, trying to get used to the change.

The mouth was different, the lips fuller, but there was no doubt she was staring into the face of her mother.

2 2

TWO DAYS LATER, with her Saturday morning shift over, she found Daniel waiting just outside the supermarket.

"Wow. I didn't recognise you. You said you'd coloured your hair, but wow! Looks great. Really great." Grace reached for the long fringe and pulled a little over her scar. No matter what the style, she insisted it stay long enough to cover the ugly injury.

"Are you still okay to go on an adventure with me today?" he asked. She nodded, though hesitantly.

"Where are we going?" she asked uncertainly. Daniel sounded mysterious when he called last night, saying he had a surprise for her. Right now, he looked like a bouncy new puppy, bright eyed and excited. Comparatively, she was dog tired after standing for hours and knew she looked a wreck. Her wrinkled button-down shirt had popped a button an hour ago, and her black nylon work pants smelled like spoiled milk, courtesy of a broken milk jug at her register. Plus, her feet were killing her. She would have preferred to go home, shower, and crawl into bed. But, she didn't want to douse the pup in cold water.

"I know you have studying to do, but it sounds like you need a bit of a break. At least for a few hours."

She hated surprises. Especially the type that meant being whisked away somewhere. That usually meant something had gone terribly wrong, and she was on the move again.

"You'll love this, I promise. It's one of my favourite places. It's really peaceful."

"Okay," she said. She was too tired to argue right now. Plus, Lowell was right. She had to live her life. She had to trust the moment. Trust Daniel. When he told her to pack some jeans, boots, and a warm jumper, she'd bundled all that into her backpack, but with the chaos of her workday, she'd forgotten about their date.

"I forgot to change. Do you mind if I duck back in and do that? Work was insane." He agreed, his eagerness exhausting her. When they finally reached his truck, the bed was covered with a tarp. That was strange. The unknown made her nervous.

"Daniel. Where are we going?" Daniel started the engine.

"It's a surprise. Really Grace, you'll love it." She didn't like the sound of this. It was happening too fast. She was losing control.

After driving an hour south, then another twenty minutes on a dirt road, Daniel parked the truck. They were over-looking an expansive field of wheat coloured grass, swaying to its own rhythm in the breeze. A line of gum trees, robust and steadfast, hugged the s-curve of the river, their leaves dancing in the wind song. Grace heard rapids flowing in the distance, the splashing water finding its own place in the river. A chill slithered down her spine, despite the warmth of the truck's cabin.

"So? What do you think? Gorgeous, right? I've been camping here since I was a kid, but no-one really knows about it."

Oh, but she did. It was all very familiar. She felt ill. Her heart raced. She couldn't think straight. Yes, she had been here before.

Daniel opened his door and came around to her side. She stared numbly into the distance. She wiped her clammy palms on her jeans. She was shivering, but not from the coldness of the winter afternoon.

"Come on, I want to show you something." She crawled out of the truck. He took her hand. She was good at hiding her emotions after years of living with her father. She was never more thankful for that skill than she was now.

With Daniel leading the way, they made their way down the trodden path toward the river. While this was public land, it was a rarely used campground and was not easily accessible. But somehow her father managed to get their rusted-out car down the rutted track. It had been a good place to hide.

Following Daniel, she remembered the couple of months they'd spent here. She'd been about fourteen. It was hot that summer, but the cool water offered a lovely respite from the heat. Her father set up a tent under the gum trees to the right of the area, hidden from vehicles coming in, but they had space there to spread out. Thankfully, Daniel was leading them off to the left. She wasn't ready to face the reality of an old home just yet.

They weaved their way through the tumbled grass toward the edge of the river, where an old hollowed-out log rested. There was a deep pocket of water just below the edge. Grace would sit on this very log for hours, stealing glances at a platypus that occasionally surfaced. She used to daydream about what was to come, once they left the river.

"Beautiful, right?" Daniel took her hand and guided her to the log. He leaned over and kissed her cheek, then looked down into the water. "My parents' place isn't far from here and it's one of those hidden gems only the locals know about. My dad and I used to camp here with friends, back when I was a kid." She let him ramble. She was stuck in her own memory lane.

"Grace?" Daniel asked, snapping her back to the present.

"Yes, it's lovely. The water looks inviting," she said, trying to divert his attention away from her. "Maybe too cold right now."

"Freezing, I bet. When I was older, I used to come here as an escape from the farm. It's peaceful and never crowded. I mean, some people camp here for weeks at a time, it's so great." He stroked her hand with his thumb as he held it in his. It's what he did. She usually found it calming, but right now, she was hoping he couldn't feel her pulse race.

"Over there is a shelf just under the water. The water

goes deep just beyond. You can sit there on that shelf and the water will cascade over your shoulders. It's like relaxing in a spa..." His voice drifted away as she remembered that shelf. She'd discovered it by accident. Her father had been in a rage one night when she didn't start the fire early enough. He punched her, knocking her against a huge gum tree. Subconsciously, she lifted and rotated her arm. That tree caused a serious bruise on her shoulder. She'd found reprieve sitting on the ledge, letting the cold water numb the pain the following morning.

"And over there," Daniel continued, 'lives...'

"A platypus," she finished absently. Daniel's head whipped around to look at her. Shit. Why did she say that? She looked over at him. He looked confused.

"I've been here before," she said, looking back to where the platypus once swam.

"You have? Seriously?" He took that as a positive and not the negative that it was.

"Yes, with my father," she mumbled.

"Grace..."

"It was a long time ago."

"Really?" He struggled to find the questions he wanted to ask. Was she ready to reveal the truth, as she had with Lowell?

"When?" he finally asked. She was silent for a while. She looked back at him, deciding she had little to lose now. Unless he was a snitch. Then she was diving in deep. She decided to brush off the creeping paranoia.

"About four years ago? We were moving. This was just one place we stopped along the way. We were here for a bit. It was before we moved to Sydney."

"A bit?" he asked. She nodded, but said nothing more. He held her hand while she told him of the places they lived, moving from place to place because of her dad's job. That was a bit of a lie, she knew. Her Dad picked up odd jobs in each new place to keep the wolf from the door. It wasn't like he was pursuing a legitimate career. Her heart boomed in her chest. She could feel her pulse pounding through her fingers. She felt deeply uncomfortable sharing this much. By the time she'd finished telling him, she was trembling.

"We should go," he said and stood.

"No, Daniel. Let's stay awhile. This is your special place. I want you to show me." She also wanted to be sure her memories stayed in the past, where they belonged.

"I don't want you to be uncomfortable, or scared, or..."

"I'm okay. This is good. Maybe it will shake off some of those demons," she said and looked back toward the water, catching a ripple in the water. The platypus had come out to say hello.

"Look. Over there," she pointed towards the water and quietened her voice to a whisper. She knew the platypus was shy, and she didn't want to scare it away. "Hello, old friend."

"You've seen him then?"

"Oh yeah. I used to sit here for hours while Dad slept off the booze. 'Pete the Platypus', I used to call him. He would bob his head up and play hide and seek with me. Pete always came out after a rough night. I used to think he was my guardian angel, popping up to check on me." Daniel squeezed her hand tightly, like he wanted to squeeze her pain away completely.

"Maybe he was?" he said, enveloping her into his arms. The platypus glided through the water, only to turn back toward them, poke his head up, then plunge back down.

"We really don't have to stay," he whispered into her hair.

"No, let's do."

"Then I'm going to get you another jumper. You're shivering." She nodded, and he leapt up and ran back to the truck, returning with another layer and a lightweight blanket.

"Thank you," she said as he wrapped the blanket around her legs. Although it was only about four in the afternoon, the sun was setting behind the surrounding hills, casting a soft glow in the fading light. He settled back beside her.

"You know, it wasn't all bad. Being here was one of the better times. Since it's too far away to get to the shops and back, he was sober for a couple of weeks. Once he dried out, he was okay to be around. He taught me how to trap rabbits and fish. Good life skills for any teenage girl to have, don't you know?" she jested, smiling at Daniel. "It was just the beginning and the end parts I'd prefer to forget."

He sat silently, letting her relive the stories at her own pace.

"We set up camp over there," she said, pointing to a cluster of gum trees. She could see the grasses were flattened around the area. Someone had made a fire ring out of river rock, closer to the water.

"We placed a tarp between two trees over our old,

battered tent. Dad found it in a garbage bin somewhere. One pole was missing, and it had a rip at one end. It leaned to the left, but it worked mostly. Dad slept outside by the fire most nights. Passed out, I suppose. And yeah, it was probably illegal to have a fire, but we always had one. I was always up at dawn, rebuilding the fire, and he'd crawl into the tent when I made too much noise. He slept in the tent all day for the first few weeks." She paused for a minute, taking a deep breath in. She looked over at the movement in the water. The platypus poked his head up again, then dived back under.

"He drank off his supply after a few weeks. He was ... well, let's just say when he realised he was running low, he got a little manic, frantically trying to work out a plan. But nothing seemed to work out, so we just stayed for a while. A few people came and went, mostly to check out the place. Usually on those days, Dad slept, and I went walking. I'd disappear for hours. Thought about running away, but I didn't have any money. I had nothing really, and we were a long way from anywhere."

"I wish I'd been here then. I would have taken you with me." She laughed.

"No, you wouldn't have. You wouldn't have looked at me twice. I looked like a wild child, born of the bush. Other than swimming in the river, I hadn't bathed, hadn't washed my hair in, God, I don't know how long. Weeks probably. With only a sliver of soap, I'm sure I stank to high heaven. I'd wash my clothes in the river too." Grace made a poor attempt at laughter when he reached over and ran his fingers through her newly blonde hair. It was shorter than it had ever been, the soft waves taking on a life of their own. Back then, her hair was a mass of greasy, curly knots.

"If only I'd known," he mumbled, then pulled her back into his arms. They sat for a long time, watching the platypus play in the water.

"Are you hungry? Figured we could eat here before we head back. I brought a bunch of stuff. Even a small grill, in case you were in the mood for a barbecue. If not, there's plenty of stuff to snack on. And I have a lantern since it gets dark fast."

"Is that what's in the back of your truck?" she asked, the tension in her neck easing a little.

"Yes," he replied.

"Yeah, you should know something," she said, smiling at him. "I really hate surprises. But I'm glad you brought me here."

"I NEED MY BIRTH CERTIFICATE." Grace lay on the floor in Lowell's lounge room with university information spread out around her. "I can't do anything without it."

"Does John have it?" Lowell asked, walking in from the kitchen, where he was preparing dinner. After conversations with Miss O'Donnell and with Daniel, she needed to figure out what was next. Her mantra of 'finish high school' was one thing, but then what? Dreaming about becoming a journalist without a plan was simply wishful thinking.

"I don't know. I remember seeing some papers laying on his bed once, but that was a while ago." What were those papers, she wondered?

"They looked official," she continued. Surely their birth certificates would be amongst the pile. She would have to go back there. Back to the apartment. She hadn't been there for weeks. She hadn't heard from her father either. Would he be out of jail by now? What if he was home when she went in? A feeling of dread filled her.

"Are you okay?" Lowell asked. He picked up the sudden shift in her mood. She'd ignore the vibe she was feeling. She needed to focus on getting her birth certificate. But what would that mean if she found it? She went by a different name now.

"It's okay. We'll go over together and find it." Lowell squeezed her shoulder reassuringly before walking back to the kitchen.

"No, I need to go by myself," she was quick to say. *Blend in*, she thought. "He doesn't know about you, remember? I want to keep it that way."

"You're not going alone Grace. That part of your life is over."

"Yeah, I know but this is something I need to do alone." If he knew about Lowell, he could find her. "Besides, I know what he's like. I know how to handle him." Lowell scoffed.

"I can handle it. If you want to wait at the corner for me, fine, but I am getting the paperwork on my own." When Lowell wouldn't give in, she finally explained to him her fears of her father finding her. He still didn't like it, but he relented.

The following afternoon, Daniel drove Lowell and Grace to her father's apartment. Grace argued she could do this alone. She didn't want either of them involved, but the pair ganged up on her. Two to one, Lowell quipped. She wasn't happy about it at first. She didn't need them there. But she had to admit, it was nice to have the support.

"I'll be five minutes. Max," she said when Daniel parked in front of the apartment block. "I am pretty sure I know where the paperwork is. If my father is out of jail, he's usually not home at this time of day. I just hope my key still works. It probably will. He's too lazy to get the locks changed. Probably wouldn't even think to do that. And I doubt the place has been leased already. Right?" She was rambling. Her frayed nerves prickled her skin, but she wanted to get this over with. She opened the door to the truck and jumped out on to the footpath, leaving her bag with them.

As she approached the door, she slowed her pace, her head bent to hear any sounds within. Things sounded quiet inside. She pushed the key in but needed to jiggle it a bit to work. It had rusted even more over the weeks she'd been away. When the lock finally clicked, she pushed the door open and was immediately assaulted by the smell of vomit and urine. She covered her mouth, but she could smell something else. That same smell she couldn't quite place before. A half empty beer bottle sat on the floor by the couch. Odd. Her father never left beer behind. Things had changed and not for the better. But the place was empty, thank God. Maybe he was still in jail and this was left over from… before.

Focus. While she'd never actually seen a copy of her birth certificate, she figured her father must have hidden it somewhere in his bedroom. With her heart in her throat, she stepped into his room, acutely aware of every sound. She looked in the cupboard and found a shirt, half hanging from a hanger. She reached to fix it, but pulled back. He'd know she'd been in the room if she did that. She took a step back to see if there was anything on the shelf above. Nothing.

A woman, yelling at her kids outside near the clotheslines, startled her.

She kept looking. Empty beer cans were strewn around, the stale liquid puddled on the stained carpet. The stench made her nauseous. She opened the top drawer of the battered chest of drawers. Shuffling through a short stack of faded shorts, she found nothing but a joint.

She tried the next drawer. There was a single t-shirt in it. She went to the bottom drawer and pulled it out. Nothing in it. Maybe there was something underneath? She pulled the drawer out all the way. Now on hands and knees, she reached into the underbelly of the dresser. Her hand touched cold metal. She recoiled from it as if it was a snake. She looked down and gasped. A muzzle pointed toward her, as if lining her up.

A gun. What the hell was her dad doing with a gun? Her eyes zeroed in. There was something laying underneath the gun. Papers. Bingo! She reached in to grab them when a loud bang hit the front door. Shit. Shit. Shit.

She hurried to return the drawer. Grace fumbled, missing the guiding rails. She tried again. It dropped in her hand. Keys scraped loudly against the lock. She heard the keys drop to the ground. Someone swore in frustration. Then a fist pounding against the door in anger. Her father. He was out of jail. Oh God.

The drawer finally caught and slid in. She looked around to make sure nothing else was out of place, then ran toward her old bedroom out of habit. Maybe she could hide there while she waited him out.

She wasn't fast enough.

"What the… What the fuck do you want?" Her father's eyes tried to focus in on her.

"I …"

He lunged at her, his hands quickly tightening around her neck, vice-like. His bloodshot eyes stared crazily at her. His breath was rank, and she noticed his bared teeth were tinged grey.

"Stop…" she squawked, but the words were halted when his fist came up hard to the side of her head. She saw stars. He released her throat and stomped away. She collapsed to the floor, gasping, trying to catch her breath.

"Look what you've done to me." His voice was laced with venom. He guzzled at the half empty bottle of beer. Draining it, he shook it, like he expected it to magically refill. When it didn't, he threw it against the wall. Glass shattered.

"That day. Remember that day? That day ruined my life. You, you little bitch. You ruined my fucking life. And then you thought you could just leave, didn't you?" She didn't know what he was talking about. Or even who he was talking about. Did he think she was her…mother? Grace flashed to the red suitcase. She tried to pick herself up. She had to get out. Her head was pounding, her throat bruised. She reached up to her neck, feeling the pain.

John stomped back over to her and picked her up by her arm, almost ripping it out of its socket.

"Where the fuck have you been? Whoring around again?" She mumbled no, but he either didn't hear her or didn't care. His hand drew back, and she reached up to push him away, but she wasn't strong enough. Whatever he was high on had given him super-powers. The force of the blow, a backhand across her face, brought blood into her mouth. She flew back, knocking over a nearby chair. Before she could think, he yanked her head back by her hair. His eyes scared her more than ever.

"What was that, bitch? Admitting you're a whore?" he slurred. John dragged his hand slowly along her torso, then bent forward, deeply inhaling her scent. "You smell like a whore."

Her blood went cold. His next punch was straight to her midsection, causing her to double over. He yanked her upright by the hair again and grabbed her crotch. He clenched. Hard. The shock stunned her.

"Giving it away to whoever wants it? Yeah, you always did that, didn't you Zoe? Fucking whore!"

He pushed her forcefully away and she tripped back-ward, over the upturned chair. Her head hit the floor with a thud. Blood spilled from her mouth. Blackness followed.

2 4

"I FIGURED I would be straight in and out. I didn't think he'd be there," Grace said, laying in the hospital bed. She had woken in a panic an hour before. Child Services would surely be called. But would they? She was over eighteen. She was an adult. No, they wouldn't be called now. She looked to Lowell, who stood next to her bed. Daniel stood at the end, clenching the bedrails. Both looked like they were trying to contain their anger. She looked back again to Lowell and narrowed in, trying to focus. She was in agony. She couldn't deal with any more rage. John had been enough. She had her own feelings to deal with. Fear mostly. Fear her father would find her again and kill her.

And yet, she still did not know how she got to the hospital.

"The last thing I remember was him pushing me, tripping over the chair."

"You're going to be okay, Jelly. You have a concussion, so you'll have a doozy of a headache for a while. A dislocated shoulder. Two broken ribs. When we came in, he was… kicking you." Lowell's eyes flicked to Daniel, but Daniel was silent, quietly seething.

She nodded. Tears began forming. She tried to brush them away.

"So, you know, nothing different from before." Lowell looked at her and tried to smile. But it was more of a snarl. The smile didn't reach his eyes. He was trying to make light of the situation. He knew how it was.

"He knocked me to the ground, kicked me in the hip, I think. That's the last I remember. He hit me a few times. Hard to the side of my head." She reached up to the bandage. The pain killers numbed her, but her head was still throbbing. "That's all I remember. Nothing until I woke up here. I don't remember you coming in."

Lowell looked at Daniel again. What was that about?

"Well, it's a good thing we did," Lowell said. Daniel gripped the end railing so hard, his knuckles were white. He'd yet to go near her, as if afraid to touch her. She didn't know what that was about. He cleared his throat.

"When can I go home?" She asked Lowell, hoping it was soon. She didn't want her father to find her here.

"I don't know. Not today at least. But, let me go ask," said Lowell, squeezing her hand for good measure.

"Daniel," she said, once Lowell left the room. He avoided her gaze. "I'm sorry you got caught up in this."

"It's not your fault, Grace." He walked toward her, pulling a chair over to the bed. "It's never your fault." She knew that and was surprised when he took her hand. Emotion hit him. He lay his head down against her leg and sobbed into the covers. What was going on? She let go of his hand and stroked his hair while he sat crying for a long time.

"They say..." Lowell walked in and stopped mid-sentence. Daniel sat up, wiped his nose across the back of his sleeve.

"Hey, it's okay. It's a lot to take in." Lowell looked to Grace. She was just as perplexed as he was.

"Yeah. Yeah, it is. I'm sorry, Grace. I didn't mean to lose it on you. It's just... when I walked in and saw you..."

Lowell jumped in.

"I'm sure seeing you laying there completely blacked out would scare anyone. Anyway, the doctors said they want to keep you overnight for observation. The police are waiting to get your statement, but I asked if they could wait until you're home before they ask you anything. They're, um, cool with it. Just need to call them when you're settled."

Daniel looked at Lowell with gratitude. Seriously, what was going on with them? Her thoughts were muddled. Was there more going on that they weren't saying? Their looks were... weird. No, she was reading into things. Lowell was always up front with her. He'd tell her if there was something going on. She was just confused. It had to be the painkillers.

"The hospital needs your details. We knew your name, address. Obviously. But they asked for your birthdate. We didn't know it. I said you were seventeen. We convinced them Daniel was your next of kin. I was going to claim it, but it's pretty clear I'm not." He smiled at her, this time more genuinely. She tried to smile back but picked up on the one thing they didn't know.

"Eighteen," she mumbled.

"What?" Lowell looked confused. "What's eighteen?"

"I am. I'm eighteen."

"When did that happen? I thought that was going to be a big event?"

"The day I moved in with you. It was my birthday."

"Geezus Jelly. Why didn't you say something?" he asked. He continued speaking, but she tuned him out. She had failed. She had no identification. No Medicare card. She'd now have to work out how to pay the hospital bill. Shit.

"I didn't get the birth certificate," she said, laying her head back in defeat against the pillow. She felt dizzy.

"Probably the least of your worries right now," mumbled Daniel.

"Where's my father now? Do you know?" she asked Lowell softly, her eyes becoming heavy. She had to know where he was. He'd find her here. But she was losing the battle to the medication.

"In jail. Where he belongs," said Daniel.

"How does she deal with it... all this bullshit? How could she put up with her father's crap for so long?" She could hear Daniel speaking as if he was far away, but her eyes wouldn't open. She could smell Lowell's aftershave in the room. He was still there too. Good.

"I feel helpless," Daniel continued. "This is worse than before." Before when? Before, when he found her at the café all bruised? Was this too much reality for him?

"I don't know if I can do this, man. She needs so much more than I can give her."

"She needs our support, Daniel," Lowell said. "Especially now. She's never mentioned this... to me, anyway. This sounds like it was the first time he tried something like this with her." First time trying what? She didn't know what Lowell was talking about. Knocked her out? No, this wasn't the first time her father had done that.

"I'm just glad the doctor gave her a sleeping pill," Daniel said.

"Yeah, maybe her mind can rest a while, too. She's been having some insane nightmares. She started telling me about them recently." Her mind flashed to the red suitcase. Then the phone. Then the gun under her father's chest of drawers. Why did he have that? It was illegal for him to have a gun. Had he used it before?

"Shit Lowell, I don't know, man. I'm so..."

"I get it. It's a lot to deal with. It's a lot for Grace, too. Now the cops are involved, it will get harder. Especially since she doesn't remember that he..."

"I just don't know if I can give her what she needs Lowell. I ..."

"What? What does that mean?" Grace heard someone pacing the room. Was it Lowell? No, he still sat beside her. She heard him breathing. It must be Daniel.

"Look, I know this is shitty, but I need to get away. Think. I need to deal with what happened. I need to..."

"Are you fucking serious right now?" Anger simmered in Lowell's voice. But there was more. Disappointment? It sounded more like disgust. Why? She was confused. What was Daniel saying? Graced willed herself to open her eyes, but the drugs were too heavy.

"Look, Lowell. I don't know what to do. I am so fucking angry I want to pull the skin from my own bones. Just beat the motherfucker to a pulp, but I can't do that. That's not right for her. I need to be strong, but I'm not sure I'm strong enough right now. I don't think I'm calm enough to help her. Right now, I want to whisk her away somewhere safe, but even then, I don't know if it's the right thing for her. I don't know what to do..." Daniel's voice cracked. "Seriously, man. I need to just get away for a bit. Think. It's just..."

"Wow. I didn't see this coming," said Lowell after a while. Or had she fallen sleep? She didn't know.

"Fuck, I'm really sorry, Lowell. I just don't know what..."

"Whatever. I'll stay with Grace. She's safe with me," Lowell said icily. She needed to ask what was going on. Come on eyes. Open. Open. Open. She could hear the words being said, but she couldn't make sense of them. "I'll do what's best for Grace..."

"Really, I'm sorry," said Daniel. He sounded a long way off.

"Whatever, Daniel. Go do what you need to do. We'll be here, sorting the shit storm out. The doctor recommended that counsellor for her. I'll get her there. One thing. Does she know about Kate?" Lowell's tone was monotone. Stone cold.

Wait what? What was the shit storm? This wasn't any different from her father's usual behaviour. A counsellor? What was that about? And who the hell is Kate?

"She knows I had a girlfriend before, but that's all she knows."

"So, she doesn't know about the suicide?" Whose suicide? Kate's?

"No," Daniel whispered. "It was never the right time." For what?

"Yeah. Sure." A chair scraped next to her, and she heard Lowell mumble, "fucking asshole." Then he left the room. Daniel came closer. His breath brushed her cheek. She felt his lips on her forehead. He was breathing faster than normal. What was going on? The pacing started again. Then silence.

Daniel whispered, "I'm sorry, Grace. It's just. Well. Lowell is a much better man than I am."

2 5

BLOOD. *Everywhere. She was running along a trail when it suddenly changed into a street. It was dark. Very dark. Lights lined the street, but it was still pitch black. Rain. Just a drizzle. Her father dragging her along. Daddy, you're hurting my arm. Then blood again. In an intricate pattern over the kitchen tile, like a spider web. Now the blood was like lava. Thick lava, flowing toward her. The nightmare changed again. Lowell was there. Jelly, he whispered. Jelly. Jelly. Jelly. She was back in the closet again. She was five. It was dark here, too. She could hear yelling. No. Screaming. Stop. Stop. Stop. She looked down at the phone. What was the number Mummy told her to call? Did she have to ring Nanny? Will Nanny come and help? She was just there today. Nanny said she'd be back. When will she be back? Is she coming before Daddy hurts Mummy? The blood again. Blood in the hallway, dribbling out of the red suitcase by the front door. The door was red too, with glass in it. There were pretty glass flowers in the door, and it was wide open. They were running down the street again. Her. And her father. Then the closet again.*

What was the number she was meant to dial? She jabbed at the phone. No. No. No. She looked at the phone again. Nanny was there. She was carrying the red suitcase. Come home to me, sweetness. You'll be safe here. Back in the closet. She held the phone again. It felt cold. Then again in the dark street, being pulled along by her wrist. A woman was pulling her now, not her father. But it wasn't her mother. And it wasn't Nanny. Who was it? Jelly. Wake up Jelly.

Her eyes flew open. Where was she? She looked around frantically. Lowell. Lowell was there. He smiled at her.

"It's okay Jelly. You were having a nightmare." He reached for her hand, but she pulled back. Why was Lowell in the nightmare? Was he there? She heard his voice.

"You. I could hear your voice," she whispered, but her voice was coarse, like she'd been screaming for hours. Her throat was dry. "Water?"

Lowell handed her a glass from the side table.

"Thank you," she said, and drained the cup. "My nightmare. It's changing."

"Changing how?" he asked as he refilled her water. She drank again. "There's a woman in it now. And I still don't know the number I'm supposed to call. I just keep looking at the phone in the closet. I don't get it. Lowell. It's like the nightmare is trying to tell me something."

"Let's worry about it later, okay? You need to rest Jelly. Do we need to ask the doctor for a sleep aid? I mean, those dreams are getting more frequent."

"I just wish I knew what they were about." They were

confusing her. So many things were going on with them. She couldn't work it out.

"Well, you're going home today. The detective who came to visit called again. She said to tell you she's coming back up to Sydney." Oh God, what did that mean?

"Why?" she asked. "Why is she coming back? I can't tell her anything more."

"Why not, Jelly? Apparently, you're eighteen now…" he smiled at her. "Thanks for telling me that, by the way. There will be hell to pay for that, you know." She flinched. "Shit. Sorry."

"I can't tell her Lowell. I just…"

"Why not Jelly? Who are you protecting? John? I can't say he's done much to protect you. Not considering…"

"Considering what?" Something nudged at her. Something Lowell and Daniel were talking about. But it was fuzzy. She couldn't put her finger on it.

"Where's Daniel?" she asked when she didn't see him. She didn't see his jacket either. She looked back at Lowell. His jaw was clenched, and his eyes were hard. He blinked, and he was instantly back to smiling, jovial Lowell. What was going on?

"He left," he said.

"Left to go home? Left for work?" She looked toward the door, expecting him to enter at any moment.

"He left. Last night. Couldn't handle seeing you in hospital. So, he left. Sorry, Jelly. Guess he wasn't as great as we thought." His voice remained flat. Grace knew Lowell's poker face.

"Suicide. Whose suicide? And who's Kate? And

married? I heard that. Is Daniel married?" Snippets of conversations came back. Things made little sense.

"What?" Lowell's face paled.

"I heard you guys talking last night. I couldn't open my eyes. It felt like they were glued shut, and I could only make out bits and pieces of your conversation. So? Who's Kate?" Lowell looked down, sighed, then looked back at her.

"How much did you hear?" he asked quietly. His eyes were wide with alarm. Why? What was going on?

"Just that. Why?"

"Doesn't matter. We were talking while you were asleep. You were out a while." He took a deep breath. "Kate is Daniel's ex-girlfriend. She committed suicide a few years ago. They found out later she was being abused by her father. That's why Daniel freaked out. He wants to save you. Wrap you in cotton wool. Protect you from the world. But you and I both know that's not reality." She nodded, but moving her head made her swimmy. There was something more. Maybe it was the drugs causing the confusion. She pulled herself up into a seated position. The room spun. Nausea teased, but after she stayed still a moment, it subsided.

"And what was the marriage thing? Did I dream that?" Lowell shook his head.

"No, we were talking about his friend Claire. She called him last night. He was telling me about how his parents had been trying to marry him off for years. I didn't realise Daniel came from a wealthy family in the Southern Highlands. Landowners. Big ones. They were trying to marry him off to Claire to merge properties.

Except Claire is gay. Daniel talked about taking you home to his parents. You know, the whole cotton wool thing. And now I know his dad is a sheep grazier, that is kind of a funny analogy. Anyway. Claire warned him about the wrath of his mother if he brought you home. His mother is a bit of a 1950s housewife, he said. Stuck in her ways." Lowell was rambling. He never rambled. Not like this.

"What is it, Lowell? What aren't you saying?" She looked right at him, but it hurt to focus. She blinked. Blinked again.

"You okay, Jelly?" He got up from his chair and walked toward the door, peered out down the hallway.

"I'm fine. Just hurts to focus," she said. "Tell me."

"We can talk about it when we get home. If they release you, that is. They may not with that banged up head of yours."

"I don't want to be here. What if my father comes and finds me?" Lowell held her eyes. He slowly shook his head.

"He won't, Jelly. He's in jail and he won't be getting out soon. The bail hearing is tomorrow. That's why the detective is coming up. It's something to do with John's arrest."

Shit. He'd blame her. He had dangerous friends. And who knew who was after them. She grabbed the covers and pulled them to the side.

"Where are you going?"

"Have to get out of here. They'll come for me," Lowell stopped her.

"No, Jelly." Lowell looked at her in disbelief.

"Why not? Why is now any different?"

"Because it is. Things have changed, Jelly. He's not getting out. You're safe here."

No, she wasn't. Her father warned of this. If he was caught, she had to run. They'd come for her. They'd find her. She had to leave. Because if she was in hospital, there would be a record of it. Of her. And they'd find her. Lowell gently took the covers from her and told her to lie back. The nausea rose fiercely this time.

"Going to be sick," she said, and he quickly handed her a container where she spilled the contents of her stomach. Lowell reached over and pressed a call button behind her to ask for help.

She buried her head into the pillows while words echoed in her head:

Bad things will happen if the truth comes out. Bad things will happen if the truth comes out. Bad things will happen if the truth comes out.

But who said those words and what did they mean?

2 6

GRACE WOKE IN A FOG. The wind howled outside, rain pounding the window. She'd had another nightmare. The details were fuzzy, but it was a feeling of dread she couldn't shake.

"Jelly? You okay?" Lowell whispered groggily from the dark lounge room.

"Bad dream. Sorry." She rolled over tentatively, aware of her broken ribs. The pain killers were wearing off. She tucked her hand under her pillow and stared out the window. She could see the shapes of the trees moving in unison. Winter was over. The world was reawakening with spring flowers, but tonight's wind would blow the buds away.

Lowell's apartment seemed bitterly cold, so she pulled the bedcovers closer. The minutes ticked by. She tried to piece the dream together. It still had elements of her normal nightmare, but something was missing. Something she couldn't work out.

Zoe. She remembered her father calling her Zoe. Her mother's name. Grace looked like her mother with her blonde hair. It'd probably been a shock for him to see her that way. She hadn't been blonde since… well, she couldn't remember when. Plus, he was clearly high. She turned slowly onto her other side, tried to close her eyes, but the pain was too intense laying like that, so she gave up and turned back to stare out the window.

"Want to talk about it?" Lowell whispered. She'd been home two days and Lowell was hovering like a mother hen. She texted Daniel but hadn't received an answer. That was odd. He usually responded quickly.

"No, it's okay. Sorry to wake you."

"You sure?" he asked. She hesitated. "I'm getting up, anyway. Can't sleep." She knew she was the reason. Maybe talking about it would help. Staring out the window wasn't resolving anything. Whatever she couldn't remember was not going away.

She heard the couch creak under his weight. He gasped when his feet touched the cold floor. When the bathroom door closed, Grace tossed away her bedcovers, then eased out of bed. She still had trouble moving too quickly. Nausea still plagued her. Standing slowly, she layered up with a jumper and walked out to the kitchen to make coffee. She stared at the clock on the stove. 5.12 a.m. Shit. Way too early.

"Okay, good. Kettle is on. Now, what's going on?" He grabbed the milk from the fridge while the kettle boiled.

"I don't know. I can't put my finger on it. It's the same nightmare. Lots of blood, thorny bushes, running. There's a woman in it." She scrunched her eyes, trying to remember. "No. Two women. One stands at the front door now. My mum, I think? She's calling to me. Telling me to come home, that I'll be safe with her. The other woman comes later in the dream. We're walking down a dark street at night. The streetlights are on and she's pulling me along by my wrist." She fell into a daze, reliving the dream.

"I try to pull away, but she keeps pulling me back to her. Like, she's wrenching my arm. I don't know who it is. But this dream is different. Then it switches again. I'm now on the floor of our old apartment. My Dad is there. He's drunk or high. He's just laid into me. I can feel the pain from the blows." She tried to take herself out of the dream, but it kept pulling her back in. "There was something about this dream, though. It felt too real. More like a memory. I don't know..." Grace shook her head, feeling a rush of pain. She braced herself on the counter while she fought the dizzy spell.

"Go sit. I'll finish the coffee." Relieved, she walked into the lounge room and curled up on Lowell's outstretched sofa bed. Minutes later, Lowell handed her a cup of hot coffee. She breathed it in like it was her lifeline.

"You're limited to two cups. Doctor's orders." She rolled her eyes. She doubted the doctor said anything about her coffee habit. Lowell was probably still on his reduction plan to get her off the stuff.

"Thanks, nag." She balanced their coffees while Lowell crawled into the bed with her and pulled the covers up around them. When he was settled, she handed him his cup.

"Okay, keep going…" He looked at her strangely. Was it… cautionary? Ignoring it, she continued back to the dream.

"This is what I know. I was at the apartment to get my birth certificate. He beat me when I was there. But in the dream, I was on the floor, crumpled like a rag doll. He was standing over me, kicking me in the ribs, screaming at me, and calling me a whore. I was… I was crying, trying to protect myself, covering my head. The next part is where it gets a little fuzzy, but the feeling. God, it feels so real." Lowell sat straighter. What? Was what she was saying just too weird? Yeah, probably. She stared into her cup, gathering her thoughts.

"He was on top of me. I remember his hands. They were rough, scratchy. He… oh…" She stopped. Lowell waited. She slowed her mind a little, remembered the details.

"His hands, they ripped at me. He was screaming at me. Calling me Zoe. I could see the spit flying out of his mouth. And his eyes, God, they were manic. He gripped his hand around my throat. I couldn't breathe. He was so rough. He was… he was pulling my pants down, ripping at my undies, as if he was about to…" She stopped talking suddenly. She looked at Lowell's face. She couldn't read his expression. She looked down. His hand squeezed the coffee cup so tight she wondered if it would shatter. She looked into his eyes again and now saw his rage.

"Lowell…" she whispered. "It's real, isn't it?" Lowell still said nothing.

"He almost…" Her voice quivered. She couldn't finish

the sentence. It was too much. Too real. Blood left her face, and she shivered. Lowell pulled her into his arms. "How did I not remember that?"

Lowell remained silent, allowing her to finish. Suddenly, she stiffened in his arms.

"You were there!" She screamed and pulled away. She ignored the pain shooting through her.

"Oh my God, Lowell. You and Daniel. You were there. How were you there? You were waiting in the truck. How did you know which apartment to go to? Oh my God, I feel sick." She dashed into the bathroom, feeling both dizzy and nauseous, but focused only on making it to the sink. When she was done vomiting, Lowell brought a damp towel to her. She mumbled thanks, wiped her mouth, and then turned the tap on, rinsing the remnants away. Lowell watched her carefully as they walked back to the lounge room. She looked around the room in a daze before crawling back to the open couch. Lowell handed her a glass of water from the kitchen.

"You saved me. Saved me from being raped by my father! Wait, Daniel. He pulled him off me. But you called the police. Oh, my God, Lowell."

"Grace..." he began. She knew it was real when he called her Grace. He only called her that when he was super serious. He moved next to her. When she looked up at him, she saw the truth in his eyes. She started shaking and sobs soon overtook her.

"He's never done that before," she rasped. Lowell pulled her into his arms, and she felt his breathing hitch as he cried with her. They held each other for a long time.

"But how..." she pulled away from him. "Did I call for you? I couldn't have." Her eyes bore into his, willing him to tell her the truth of what happened. She had to know everything now. He got up and returned with the box of tissues from the bathroom. He held one out to her without saying a word.

"Snot. Gross." She took a tissue, blew her nose. He walked into the kitchen and made more coffee, then settled in again next to her.

"Thanks," she said, taking a sip from her mug. She waited for him to answer.

"We were waiting in the truck, as planned, but you were taking too long," he said, pulling the blanket up around them. "We went to see if you were okay." Grace held his gaze. She needed to face whatever he told her. But before he could continue, more of the day came back to her.

"I remember him screaming at me. His fists were hard, like rocks. He kept saying: 'What did you do?' And he kept saying my mother's name, Zoe. Over and over. But I have no clue why he said that, or what she ever did to him." It was all rushing back to her now.

"I went to get my birth certificate. I looked for it in his bedroom. The drawer fell out. I thought I'd never get it back in. I thought the place was empty, but he must have come back. It was too quiet for him to be home. And, God did the place stink. Wait. You know that part. You were there. Anyway, when he saw me, he just... lunged for me. His eyes. They were, I don't know, bloodshot, but his pupils were like pinpricks. He was high. Probably for days. He left a half-drunk bottle of beer... I should have known. He's a mean drunk, but he's terrifying when he's high."

"The smell. I remember it hit me as soon as I walked through the door. Vomit. Urine. And something else."

"Meth," said Lowell.

"Yeah. I wondered," she said, the memories flooding back. "He dragged me around the room by my hair. I begged him to let me go, but he threw me. He screamed at me and, yeah, that's when I got a whack to the head. I heard a crack, but I may have hit the table as I went down. I'm not sure." Grace continued talking, infusing pieces from that day with pieces of her past that she'd never considered before.

"The nightmares have been more frequent lately. But it's hazy. What's real and what's the nightmare? I mean, there are things I don't remember from when I was young. There are also things I questioned back then, but I was too little to speak up. Like, why was it okay to lock a seven-year-old in the house for three days while he went out partying? I dream about running through thorns, scratchy bushes. In every nightmare, I'm running through bushes. I think that was real. I remember my arm dislocating when he pulled at it while we were running. I don't think I was going fast enough. But I was young then. Like, five? And that woman, walking me down a street at night, holding my wrist? I was pulling away. She was real too, I think. I remember being locked in a room by her. I think she came later. Maybe when I was seven or eight?"

"Wait," she said, repositioning herself to get comfortable. "What happened to me after…" Grace couldn't even finish the sentence. She inched her way off the couch and started pacing. She knew she was all over the place. Her memories. Her words. But now her anger was building, too. She felt like a dam had burst in her mind and she couldn't control the flood.

"You were unconscious when we found you. When I called emergency, they sent both police and an ambulance. They took you to the hospital..." She opened her mouth to say something, but he added quickly, "They did some routine tests, nothing invasive."

"You were unconscious for a while. They were concerned. Your father had seriously used you as his punching bag."

"Yes. I remember waking to find my ribs were taped."

"They asked us about that. They said there were old injuries," she nodded. That sounded about right. "Daniel and I were questioned by the police at the hospital."

Grace stopped moving. Her face went grey.

"When the police arrived, John was out cold on the floor. Daniel decked him, but we didn't tell the police that. Anyway, John's pants were still down around his ankles. When the police went to rouse him, he came up swinging. Took a swipe at a police officer. One cop went around taking photos while another collected evidence. There was a lot of blood." Grace sat back down. Lowell brought the bedcovers up around her.

"What happened after that?"

"Once you were settled at the hospital, we went to the police station and finished filing the report. They filed some other charges against him. Possession. Assaulting a police officer. Attempted rape. Assault against you. When you came to, you didn't remember what had happened.

They told us to just let the memories return naturally." She nodded, but something still wasn't clicking.

"I just don't get what he was talking about. He was calling me a shacked-up whore," Grace said, remembering. She looked at Lowell. "Some of it makes no sense."

GRACE FINALLY EXHAUSTED herself a few hours later. Her headache had turned into a migraine, so Lowell gave her a painkiller the doctor prescribed, then tucked her into bed. She knew she needed sleep. She was all over the place, and the memories were just getting more and more jumbled. What was real? She didn't know anymore. Everything hurt. Lowell told her he was going out while she slept. She was asleep before the front door even closed.

When she woke, the aroma of something amazing wafted from the kitchen. She carefully got out of bed, found the jumper she'd been wearing earlier, and headed out to investigate what smelled so good.

"Hey, Jelly," Lowell said, looking up as he unloaded container after container from a paper sack. There was a gigantic bouquet of daisies on the side table, a gift-wrapped box on the couch, and a decadent cake sitting on the kitchen counter.

"Hi. What's all that?"

"Thai food. Bland stuff though. Wasn't sure what you could eat. I ordered in. I'm sure you're hungry." Her stomach rumbled at the sight of the food.

She gestured to the flowers, the wrapped gift, and then pointed to the cake.

"And all that?"

"Well, since you didn't tell me about your birthday, I thought we'd have a little celebration. I would have made the cake myself, but I didn't want to wake you." She was gobsmacked. No one had bought her a cake before, let alone made one. Well, not since her mother died.

"But first, well, sorry to spring this on you, but Daniel was here earlier. He's coming back in, oh," he glanced at the clock on the wall, "five minutes. Sorry, figured you'd be up before now."

"Oh. God, I'm sure I look like…" she said, raking her fingers through her knotted hair.

"To be honest, I don't think he cares what you look like, but maybe brush your teeth?" He gave her his usual cheeky smile. It settled her.

"Did he say why he's coming? Or maybe the question should be, why he left?"

"All I know is he's been a shit. I won't excuse him for that, but I guess you should hear him out."

"Maybe," she said, and headed to the bathroom. She looked in the mirror. She had an imposing black eye, and a purple bruise that spread up and around her cheek. She put her hands to her hair. It was sticking straight up on one side, like a lopsided cockatoo.

"I'm going to have a shower," she yelled out to Lowell.

"Yell, if you need help. I'll send Daniel in when he gets

here," Lowell teased. She was happy to see he was back to normal. Still, she didn't need Daniel in here helping her. They hadn't moved past kissing, so there was no way she was going to let him see her naked now. Especially if he'd already seen… No. Don't think about it. She tried to get the image of the attack out of her head. Easing out of the oversized shirt Lowell had loaned her, she knew the shower would be a slow process. But she'd manage it. She had before.

Fifteen minutes later, she walked out to the kitchen, clean and refreshed. She wore Lowell's Bon Jovi t-shirt over polka dotted pyjama bottoms. Daniel stood, looking very uncomfortable, near the doorway. A butterfly tape crossed his cheek, and he was also sporting quite the black eye. He held a bouquet at his side.

"Holy crap," he said. "Sorry, hi." He looked sheepish. "These are for you," holding the flowers out to her.

"Hi Daniel. I could say the same about you. What happened to your face?" she asked, looking at his cheek, avoiding his gaze.

"Stupidity. Got into a squabble at the pub near my parent's place. I picked a fight with a known troublemaker. Doesn't matter. How are you feeling?" He shoved his hands deep into his front pockets. She looked him over. He wore the usual jeans and boots with a soft blue button-down shirt. Today, he looked like a rich grazier's son.

She ran her hand through her hair, pulling one strand in front of her scar. His nervousness made her uncomfortable. He looked like he didn't want to be there. Lowell stepped forward and took the flowers from her and placed them on the kitchen counter.

"Crap," said Lowell. "I forgot something from my car. I'll be back in a few minutes." She knew he was escaping to give them a few moments alone. He was as transparent as a brick wall.

"Why did you leave?" she asked, cutting to the chase. She didn't like that he'd left suddenly without telling her why. Especially leaving it for Lowell to explain. But she wouldn't clue him in on that.

"Lowell said you remember what happened?" Grace nodded. He hesitated and began pulling his shirt away from his chest, like the room was too hot. It wasn't.

"I got scared. I was so angry. God, I just wanted to kill the fucker and then I looked at how broken you were. How you didn't remember, and yeah, I freaked out."

"So, you made it all about you?" She knew all about anger, too.

"Yeah. I owe you an apology. I fucked up. I was angry at your dad and confused, I suppose. I didn't know how to help you."

"Sure." She wasn't sure he knew any better. It must be nice to have the ability to switch off when things got hard. Talk about privileged!

"I just needed to clear my head, I guess. To take a breath. It was just... all too much."

"Welcome to my life, Daniel." He looked at her with pain in his eyes. She was surprised to not feel any sympathy for him. Instead, she felt... what? She didn't know.

"I didn't expect to find you on the floor. I thought you were dead."

God, she was tired of men making things all about

them. Her father. Lowell's father. Now Daniel. She spun on her heel in disgust, but dizziness overcame her. He caught her under the arm as her knees buckled.

"Take it slowly. Where are you needing to go?"

"Couch," she said, hating the fact she needed help. Daniel seemed off. She didn't think it was the meds clouding her judgement. He just seemed sad and ... disconnected. Lowell mentioned his ex-girlfriend, but she wanted to hear the story directly from him. Daniel guided her to the couch, but he continued to stand.

"Do you want to tell me about Kate?" His face registered his shock. "I heard you talking to Lowell when I was in hospital, but I couldn't open my eyes. The pain meds have been doing weird things to me. I've never been on them before. It really throws you off kilter."

"Never? Even with the past beatings from your dad?"

"No," she said, wondering if he was avoiding the subject. "The times I've been in hospital, I've left before they gave me anything. My dad, well, he wasn't a fan of hospitals." Daniel shook his head slowly.

"You grew up in a different world than me, that's for sure," he said. "My Mum used to give me painkillers after playing football on Saturdays."

"So, Kate? Or are you avoiding that question too?"

"Yeah." He blew out a breath and took a seat next to her. "Kate and I went out for a while, a couple of years ago now." He went quiet, rubbed his hand over his hair. He put his face in his hands, then rubbed that too, careful not to bump the cut on his face. Grace kept quiet, letting him gather himself. But she wouldn't wait long for him to explain.

"Every time I think of Kate, I want to cry. I'm not kidding. Kate had a story all her own." Daniel ran his fingers through his hair again. Clearly a nervous gesture she'd not noticed before.

"After going out for about six months, we, um, slept together. Afterward, Kate turned into a sobbing mess. I didn't know what was going on. She was hysterical, and it took ages for her to calm down, to tell me what was going on. That's when she told me she'd been sexually abused by her father. We talked for hours, and she decided she was going to press charges. I was going to go with her to the police. You know, support her. Except, the next day, before I could pick her up to go to the police station, her mother found her with a suicide note next to her body. She'd taken pills. It had been too much for her."

"God, that's horrible. The poor girl," she said and meant every word, but it didn't explain Daniel's running.

"And you thought that happened to me and that I'd react the same way as Kate?"

"Yeah, I think I did. I had a lot of therapy after… that. I read a bunch of books about sexual abuse, and about how people don't really recover all the way from it, if it happens during childhood. Some find a way to move forward, eventually. Others break, like Kate did. I got scared because I couldn't protect you. I know, it's irrational."

"Yes, it really kind of is."

"Last night, my friend Claire and I had a long chat about what happened and why I fled. She calls it my white knight syndrome. When I told her about you, she questioned my motives for why I was going out with you. She asked me if I was trying to make up for Kate. To be fair, I'm not altogether sure that my feelings for you, at the start anyway, weren't somehow connected to what happened with Kate. Especially when I saw the bruises in the café. I wanted to make sure you were safe."

"Wow," she was shocked. She thought there was something between them. But that's all she was? A do-over?

"I don't feel that way anymore. I guess I'm in awe of you. You're so independent. The way you have pulled yourself out of your own situation. To get past what's happened to you. To make a better life for yourself. You're determined. And I really like that about you." Was this an apology? She wasn't sure what to make of it. She wasn't Kate. Nor were the situations the same. But they could have been. She could have been raped by her father. She could have died. But would she have committed suicide, thinking she had no other way out? No, she didn't think so.

"I've had this thought lately," she said eventually. "This situation wasn't caused by me. Or by something I did. This is my father's story. And I am in control of my own. Am I confused about my past? Sure. Am I hurt by what happened? Yes, of course. But I guess I'm angry most of all. Enraged, really. I want to know why my father did what he did. He at least owes me that much."

"I think we all want to know the answer to that." Sure, she thought, but Daniel didn't know her whole story.

When Daniel left, Grace stood at the door and realised any romantic relationship between them was over. She couldn't deal with his baggage and her own. She was sad to think about it. Most of all, she was sad if she lost him as a friend. She didn't have many of those, and he had saved her from her father. But the feeling of disappointment was palpable, knowing he may not be there when she needed him most. She needed people she could count on if she was going to come out of this okay, not more disappointment.

"Come on Jelly, you need to open your gift," said Lowell, bringing her out of her thoughts. He invited Daniel to stay since the icy vibe in the room had thawed a little, but Daniel made his excuses and left. She was kind of glad, if she was honest with herself. His leaving her at the hospital had tarnished the silver on his armour. Claire hit the nail on the head with that description. White knight indeed.

Now, a huge box wrapped in blue paper and a flurry of ribbon sat on her lap.

"Damn. Where did you learn how to wrap a gift?" Grace asked Lowell, bemusement written all over her face. "I hope you know that if you ever get a gift actually wrapped from me, consider yourself very lucky. But then it will probably be wrapped in newspaper, so..."

"I learned from an old boyfriend named Frank. He had many talents. Gift wrapping was only one of them. Now, open it!"

She carefully removed the ribbon and cleanly undid the tape from the paper. Seeing the end of the box inside, she gasped and stopped unwrapping.

"Is it what the box says it is?"

"Keep unwrapping and you will find out." She did,

going as fast as she could to find the treasure inside. Squealing, she hugged Lowell ferociously.

"Are you serious? A MacBook Air? I can't! Oh Lowell. Really?" She picked the computer out of box carefully and hugged it. "Oh, my God."

"Well, I'm glad you like it. Mumma contributed, saying it was her way of saying thank you," Lowell said, smiling. "And I'm sure it will come in handy, Miss Journalism Major. We send you successfully on your merry way to university."

Grace hugged him again. Pulling back from the hug, she locked eyes with him.

"Thank you, Lowell. You are..." she said, tearing up. She cleared her throat. "You are the best person I know. But are you sure? This is a lot."

"Grace, you have given me more than you will ever know. This is only a small token."

FOUR DAYS AFTER THE ATTACK, Grace pulled out a notepad and started writing. She needed to offload all the thoughts swirling in her head. Lowell left her to teach his classes. She was glad for the space and, now with a laptop of her own, she was eager to do some research.

Lowell arrived home later to find Grace staring intently at the laptop screen.

"Jelly? Are you okay?" She looked up, took a moment to focus. She blinked several times to clear her burning eyes.

"Hi. Yes. I think so. Here, I need to show you something." Lowell came around the couch and sat beside her.

"I've been writing. I decided to change my English assignment from the human rights focus. I emailed Miss O'Donnell and told her what happened, asking if it was okay to change at this late date. She checked for me and said, 'under the circumstances' it's fine. So now, I've written about living with my father. I had to get it out."

"Okay. That's good." He seemed circumspect, but supportive.

"Maybe. I mean, it took me weeks and weeks to write the women's rights piece, and it's only taken a few hours to write about this."

"Well, you know about this first-hand."

"Yes, but I still needed to do some research. Look." Grace turned away, picked up her notepad. It was full of notes.

"I listed everything I can remember. But it's odd. There are so many gaps. Things aren't adding up. He's been violent for as long as I can remember. Not toward me at first, he was rather nice to me for a while. But he was always angry with her. Keep in mind, I was young. But that came back to me today." Grace was going a mile a minute now.

"Dad told me my mum died of cancer, but that's not what the detective said. I remember her being afraid of doctors. She always wore long sleeves. I don't remember her ever wearing a dress or t-shirt. She was scared of him. That was another thing I didn't remember until today. There's another part where I'm drawing a blank. The night my mother died. I was five, I know that. And I know now that the last memory I have of her was that night. The night in my nightmares. I remember hiding in the closet, hearing her screams, the phone in my hand, unsure of what number to call. That's what my nightmares are always about. I am reliving that night. And I watched him..." her voice fell to a whisper, "rape her."

Grace felt bile rise in her throat. She jumped up and raced to the bathroom, relieved to reach the toilet in time.

Lowell followed her in, then handed her a damp cloth when her stomach was empty.

"Grace. Stop a while. You need ..." She shook her head.

"There's more." She dashed back into the living room to find her notes. She flipped a page. She wasn't stopping now.

"I dug more deeply. I think my last name is Pruitt, not Thompson. My mother's name was Zoe. She was a model. I think my name is Grace Pruitt." She felt frantic, like a freight train was coming at her at full speed and her feet were stuck. She put her hand over her pounding heart, something she always did when it was racing like this, hoping to ease the stress. But it was an empty gesture.

"Okay. Take a breath. Let's slow down a bit. One thing at a time. Come on, let's get you some water." Lowell led them to the kitchen.

"Sorry," she said. "Nothing says friendship more than watching someone vomit."

Lowell laughed. "Don't be sorry. I was about to push you aside! I hate watching people vomit." She rolled her eyes. She wasn't completely lost in what was happening to her. This affected him too, probably brought back memories of issues with his own dad. He handed her a glass of water, and she took a long drink.

"Are you okay? Really Jelly. Are you?"

"Yeah. I think so. It's just..."

"Yeah. It is just. It's a lot to process. A lot to discover. Geezus, Jelly, how did you even work that out?"

"Some stuff the detective said. Like, the tattoo my dad has. Or, when she mentioned murder? I don't understand what she meant by that. I mean, I don't remember how my mother died. Maybe it wasn't cancer after all, like my dad said. I'm remembering bits from around that time. I think my nightmares are true. Like, they're trying to tell me something." She started pacing like a greyhound going around a track, chasing the rabbit it would never reach.

"Need a break from it?" he asked. She shook her head.

"No. It's like everything is coming at me at all at once and every nightmare I've had is finally making sense." They walked back into the lounge room and sat down in front of the computer.

"The red suitcase. You've mentioned that a lot."

"Yeah. The detective mentioned that. I think mum and I were leaving my dad that night. Maybe he came home earlier than she expected? I had a dream once of Nanny, my grandmother, saying *'Come home to me, sweetness. You'll be safe here.'* I dreamt my mother said it to me, too. She was standing at the front door, next to that suitcase." Grace, as if mesmerised, stared off toward the darkening street outside.

"The suitcase, it was by the front door. Her handbag was on top. I remember my backpack too." She smiled. "It was a 'Dora, The Explorer' backpack my mum bought me. I had that with me for years. Mum used to call me Dora as a pet name because I always wanted to explore. I was always hiding in cupboards or dressing rooms. I remember she lost me one time at some markets. It was in... Melbourne. Yeah... It was because I noticed a toy I wanted, and I wanted to go look. God, she was frantic. I remember how crazy she looked when she found me but, not long after she did, my father showed up and screamed at her.

Called her a stupid bitch, then dragged her out of the markets."

"And you think John killed your mother?" Lowell asked. She smiled, then realised she'd have to explain her odd reaction to his bold question.

"Sorry, but I just realised something. You never call him my dad. Or my father. Only John."

"Yes. Because a parent doesn't do what he's done. Not if he loves them," he answered. "Now, back to the point. Do you think he killed your mum?"

"I don't know." She paused, seeing images of them on the floor in the kitchen. She shook her head, shaking off the sticky image. "Yes, I think so. I don't know. I don't remember him killing her. Only…" She took in a deep gulp of air, her breath ragged and filled with emotion. She tried to smooth the rough edges of her nails down. She was working on stopping the obsession.

"Right," said Lowell simply.

"I don't remember what happened next. I keep trying to work out what's true in the dreams. Running through the bush with thorns scratching my arms. I mean, I remember him screaming for me to run. I remember that. I remember him pulling me along. Hard enough that it dislocated my arm. I remember screaming at the top of my lungs, then his hand covering my mouth before he popped it back in. I remember deep scratches on my arms but I'm not sure if that was then. Maybe it was later?" She looked down at her arms and ran her hand along them, as if the raised lines of torn flesh remained. "I remember staying in a motel that night by the highway. It had bedbugs."

"Okay. So, why do you think your name is Grace Pruitt and not Thompson?"

"Because I know that with every move, my father changed our name. Never my first name. He told me, when I was little, that I was too stupid to keep track of two names. So, my first name always remained the same."

"That would also explain why you've never seen your birth certificate." Grace nodded, her mind racing back to the papers and the gun she'd discovered under the dresser. Were they still there? She'd hadn't told Lowell that part. It was just too confronting for her to imagine why her father would even have a gun.

"Look, this is what I found." She turned the laptop around so he could clearly see the screen. It showed a page with the names John and Grace Pruitt in the article. A picture of a very young Grace and a rather rough-looking John appeared midway down. A photo of her mother from her modelling days appeared at the bottom. Seeing the photo of her mother had been like looking in a mirror. No wonder her father had been confused.

"Whoa, you really look like her," Lowell said.

"There's more." She clicked back and then opened another article.

The title read: ZOE PRUITT, DEAD. HUSBAND AND CHILD GO MISSING.

29

THEY BOTH JUMPED at the knock on the door. Grace's eyes went to the clock. It was just after eight, but it felt so much later. Panic filled her. What if her father had gotten out of jail? She wouldn't put it past him. She looked at Lowell and hoped he understood her next move.

"I'm hiding. In case it's him," she whispered, then grabbed her notebook, the laptop and ran to hide behind the door in the bathroom. It was a stupid place to hide, but there was nowhere else in the tiny space. It would have to do.

"Jelly. What are you doing?" he whispered from the bathroom's doorway. The knock at the door became more insistent.

"Hiding. Go see who it is. I'm… I'm scared, Lowell. I don't want him to find me." She shooed him away. Shaking his head, he went to the door. There was a pause, then she heard the door open. Grace sucked in a breath.

"Detective. Hello." The detective? Wait. Lowell said

something about her returning to Sydney. Her mind whizzed. She's from Melbourne. Her mother. Dead. Is she? What was real?

"May I come in? I'm looking for Grace. The hospital said they released her and she's in your care?"

"Um, yes, please, come in." Shit. Shit. Shit. Shit. She should have closed the bathroom door. She heard the front door close, and Lowell offered the Detective and… someone else, a drink. Someone else? Who else was here? She heard Lowell stalling. Should she go out? She could ask the detective some questions. No. That would reveal she knew something more. Maybe she could just hear what the detective had to say? A cold case, she said she was working on. She knew about her father's tattoo. The crow. It was very unusual. Distinctive, the detective called it. She was right. But who was the other person with her?

Lowell offered them a seat on the couch. Shit.

She took a deep breath. She had to do this. She flinched when she saw her bruised face in the mirror. She mouthed 'you can do this' at her reflection, then stood tall and walked out into the lounge room.

Sitting next to the detective was a stocky man in a light grey suit. He looked older, maybe in his sixties, with hair greying at the temples. She'd seen him before. Where? Her mind raced, then zoomed in like a spotlight in the dark. He was talking to the motel clerk where they'd stayed that first night. The place with the bedbugs. They left quickly after her father had seen the man. She had her Dora backpack with her. The man sitting on Lowell's couch was the man they'd been running from. Shit. Shit. Shit.

She wanted to run.

"Grace. Hello, it's nice to see you. This is Detective Grant from the Melbourne office. My superior. We wanted to follow up with you on some questions." Grace stared at the man. He stared right back, his eyes taking in every inch of her.

"Hello, Grace. It's nice to finally meet you. We've been looking for you a long time."

Detective O'Neal shot a look at him. It caught his attention, and he smiled at his colleague.

"Yes, it's her."

Grace's heart leapt into her throat. What did he mean 'her?'. And what did he mean he was looking for her for a long time? Lowell touched her back softly. She jumped.

"Jelly. It's okay. You're okay," he said.

"Please, Grace, have a seat," Detective Grant said, offering her a seat on the couch. Grace shook her head. It was the last place she wanted to be. The detective folded his arms in front of him and remained standing as well.

"I'm sure you have a lot of questions. And, we have information we would like to share with you." Lowell shot the detective a look of suspicion. Good. She needed him on her side, relieved now to have shared her past with him. His Dad's nefarious connections made Lowell just as wary of the police as she was.

"We know you've been through a lot, particularly the last few days," Detective O'Neal said. She smiled empathetically. She seemed genuine, but Grace wasn't quite sure. "We're not here to hurt you, Grace. Just the opposite in fact. We want to protect you. You're safe from your father now. We believe we have information that will help you." She looked back at Lowell. His face changed from wariness to hope. She shook her head. She didn't believe she was safe. Not with this strange man in the room. The man who'd been chasing them all these years. *Who was he?*

"Maybe we should listen to what they have to say?" Lowell said quietly, then leaned in and whispered in her ear. "You're not going anywhere with them, Jelly, I promise. I've got you." Grace nervously picked at her cuticles and continued to stand, ready to flee if she had to.

"As you know, we're holding your father in custody. His name is not John Thompson, as we thought." She studied Grace's face for any sign of surprise and continued when Grace remained stoic.

"After the murder, your father took you and ran." Grace jolted upright.

"Murder?" asked Grace, nearly inaudible. The newspaper article was true then. Detective O'Neal nodded. Grace could feel Detective Grant watching her reactions. She picked her cuticles harder and lowered her head when she felt blood on her fingertips. Lowell walked over to the console table by the front door, grabbed a tissue, then handed it to her. She wrapped the tissue around her bloodied finger. Lowell reached over and took her free hand in his.

"Yes, Grace, I'm afraid your mother was murdered," Detective O'Neal said. Grace was quiet for a few minutes. She needed to process this. The articles online were right.

"Your father's name is Michael Pruitt." She jumped when Detective Grant took over the narrative in a gravelly baritone. He took a seat beside Detective O'Neal on the couch.

"We know he changed your last name frequently. We also know he kept your first name the same, but changed his name to John quickly. We are assuming you know that much, since you have had several names over the years. We figured out that your father moved about every six months?" The statement came out as a question. Grace didn't move. She didn't confirm their suspicions or deny them. The detective continued. "You're originally from Melbourne. Your mum, Zoe, was twenty-nine when she died. She was murdered, but we'll spare you the details."

"She was a model," Detective O'Neal said, picking up the thread, then pulled a file from her bag resting against the couch. "She was very much in demand until she married your father. Your mother came from a wealthy family in Melbourne. Your grandmother has put a lot of money into trying to find you." Grace tried to remain passive, but her wide eyes betrayed her surprise.

"Come home to me, sweetness. You'll be safe here," Grace whispered.

"Pardon?" asked Detective Grant. His eyes drilled into hers.

"That's what Nanny told Mummy," she said before realising she'd spoken aloud. Grace remembered the day Nanny gave her the Raggedy Ann doll. something. Nanny took the doll and pointed to the hand-stitched heart under the dress. She whispered she'd made the doll especially for Grace, and put her own heart into it. She told her the doll would protect her and it would wrap her in love, always. Grace loved that doll.

Could she trust their information? It confirmed what

she'd read. Confirmed what she knew, especially what she'd pieced together that afternoon. She lunged ahead.

"I thought I only dreamt those words, someone saying those words to me, but my Nanny said them. She wanted to…"

"Save you. Both of you. Yes," said Detective O'Neal.

"So, Nanny is still alive?" Grace dared to ask. Both detectives nodded. She felt the lump in her throat.

"Alive …" she whispered.

"And eager to speak with you. I promised her I would call immediately when we found you," Detective Grant said. "And I will call her tonight. She will want to speak with you, of course."

Grace nodded. She was numb. All of this new information was too overwhelming.

"She never gave up on finding you," Detective O'Neal said. "She paid for my trip to Sydney when I was here last time. We didn't know then if it was you. We wanted to be sure."

"But first Grace, your father is facing a lot of charges," Detective Grant said bluntly. "He's accused of alleged identity fraud, larceny, drug dealing and more. He'll be incarcerated for certain, and for a long time, I imagine."

"But not murder?" asked Lowell. He nudged Grace and suggested they sit on the floor, but Detective Grant got up and offered his seat to Grace. She eyed him suspiciously but took the seat next to Detective O'Neal.

"No, not murder at this time. We're still investigating. It's not, well, open and shut as they say in the movies," said Detective O'Neal.

"You don't trust me, Grace," Detective Grant said. Oh,

he was right about that. The detective remained standing, looking down at her. Lowell took a seat on the edge of the couch, close to Grace. He wasn't leaving her, as promised. Grace looked up at Detective Grant and shook her head.

"No. I've seen you before. We ran from you," she said, meeting his gaze.

"I understand your hesitation. Let me explain," he said, then surprised her by sitting on the floor opposite her.

"Your father worked for me as a police informant. I knew him as Michael. Mike actually."

"He worked… undercover?" she asked. That made little sense.

"No, not like that. He was mixed in with a dangerous crowd in Melbourne. He was known in their organisation as The Crow."

"Because of his tattoo," added Detective O'Neal. She pulled a photo from a file. The detective showed Grace an old, blown-up photograph of a man who looked much like her father. He was shirtless, with a large black crow tattoo on his left shoulder. It was taken at a distance, but the tattoo stood out. It was exactly like her father's.

"That photo was taken by me about nineteen years ago. The, ah, organisation he was involved in, would send The Crow in if they needed to clean up criminal evidence. He worked as a landscaper, so it was a great cover. Moving from job to job was good for the organisation, and me."

"After your mother's murder, we lost sight of your father. We only knew that he was still in Melbourne. He had broken ties with the organisation, and he wasn't checking in with us." Lowell gently squeezed her shoulder. He had to know this was hard to hear.

"I'm sure it's a shock to you, Grace," said Detective O'Neal. Her eyes were kind, but Grace wondered if this was a good cop, bad cop scenario. She looked down at Detective O'Neal's file. She saw the corner of another image peeking out.

"Do you have any photos? Of her, before she died?" Grace asked. She couldn't say her mother's name to these people. Detective O'Neal reached in and pulled two photos out. The detective handed her a headshot. There was her mother. Her hair was blonde, shoulder length. Her eyes were the same colour as Grace's, a kind of sage green. Her cheekbones were defined like Grace's, too. She touched her mother's face.

"You look just like her, Jelly," Lowell said quietly, and she nodded, slowly. "It's no wonder he called you Zoe." Grace stiffened.

"What was that?" asked Detective Grant.

Grace looked up at the detective, her fingers still tracing her mother's face. She opened her mouth, then closed it. Looking down at the photo of her mother, she heard her mother's voice in her head, *You're safe now, baby*. They were the same words her Nanny used, but she could hear her mother's voice clearly. It was as if her mother was speaking directly to her. She looked back at the detective, then up at Lowell. He smiled at her with reassurance. Lowell got up and made them all coffee while she told him what she remembered of her father's attack.

. . .

"There are some things I don't understand," Grace said, looking down at the photo she couldn't part with. She looked up at Detective O'Neal.

"What are they? Maybe we can join the dots for you. It was a long time ago," she said and took a sip of coffee.

"That night. The night she died. I remember running with my father. He seemed frantic. Desperate to get away. Wanting to leave quickly. He kept saying to my mother that night, 'what did you do?' He kept repeating it. I remember she was terrified. But I was young. And… I keep having these nightmares, but now I don't know where the dreams end and where reality begins."

"I'll answer that one. Or at least speculate on why he said that. Around the time of your mum's death, we learned that the organisation found out that your father was informing for us. We don't know if your mother was killed in retaliation or whether your father killed her. We don't think your mother knew about what your father was caught up in. But I think she suspected. She filed an AVO on your father that afternoon," Detective Grant said.

"An AVO?" Grace asked, confused.

"Ah, an Apprehended Violence Order. It's filed to protect victims of domestic violence. When people don't feel safe or have been threatened by someone."

"It's what we filed on my father at the time of my mum's attack, remember?" said Lowell, softly. Yes. She remembered that now.

"Your father was working that afternoon. His land-scaping business was legit, so the police tracked him down easily. I got wind of the AVO, but I couldn't stop it from being served. Your father went back to the organisation's compound afterwards, but later, he disappeared. I suspect he went to find your mother."

"That explains the suitcase by the door. We were leaving. My mother and I," Grace said. Detective Grant nodded.

"Because of the AVO, your father was exposed. The organisation didn't like that."

"Was he into drugs back then?" Grace asked.

"Yes. That's how your father got mixed up with them originally. He started using, then became a dealer to support his habit. He dug himself a hole he couldn't get out of when he fell into debt with the wrong people."

Detective O'Neal added, "Your dad became a victim of his addiction. Early on, your dad was a solid member of the community. He owned a very successful business. One of his clients was a friend of your mother's. That's how they met. Soon after they married, he took on a client who was mixed up with the organisation. That's when your dad got involved in drugs. For years, your grandmother tried to get you and your mother away from it all."

"But by then, he was involved with us, too," said Detective Grant. "He was pretty desperate."

"He got clean once or twice. He was a better father during those times. Taught me how to play the guitar. Taught me how to read and write." She laughed. "He would rap me over the knuckles if I got lazy with my writing. Said that I could do anything, be anything. Except…"

"That's hard to do when you're on the run. It's hard to know who you are, what you are capable of, when you're scared all the time," said Detective Grant. He looked at her with kindness. Maybe he wasn't all bad.

"The organisation you mentioned… are they still after him? I know we were running from someone, something. I thought it was…" she looked quickly to Detective Grant.

"Me? No, I would have protected your father. He was a good informant. We took the cell down about five years ago. I can't promise you your dad will be safe when we get back to Melbourne, but we'll do our best to protect him. He pissed off a lot of nasty people." This shocked her. Had she just killed her father by telling them what she knew? She took in a deep rattly breath, but no air reached her lungs. Emotion threatened to overwhelm her.

"Hey, Jelly. It's okay. You did what you had to do." Lowell said, rubbing her back. "Think of my father. Not all fathers are great. Some shouldn't even be fathers. He may have been good occasionally but think about it. He's fucked up, Jelly. One day he's buying you Chinese. The next he's beating you to a pulp. Not to mention the other night…"

"There was another woman," she said, visions flying through her head. "In my nightmares she was always dragging me down a dark street," Grace asked.

"Ruth Smith, I think. She was part of the organisation. She was arrested about ten years ago for child abuse," Detective Grant said. Grace nodded. Yeah, she never had a good feeling about that woman.

"What I don't understand…" Detective Grant eventually said, after giving her space to process. "Or rather, what's been bothering me all these years, is why your father took you with him. Your grandmother would have taken care of you. It would have been far easier if he left you behind."

Bad things will happen if the truth comes out.

Who said that? Her father? She shook off the thought. She had to trust herself, trust these people. She'd learned to trust Lowell over the last year. She'd even briefly trusted Daniel, but she didn't want to think of that disappointment. That was Daniel's baggage, not hers. No, she had to trust that she could handle whatever truth she learned. Her father couldn't hurt her now. He's in jail, she reminded herself. And if it was this detective they were running from, well, he was providing answers her father refused to provide. She realised now her father had been lying to her for years. Why?

"I have been writing some things down," said Grace. "Things I remember."

"Oh?" said Detective O'Neal. Grace knew this was what the detective had been waiting for. She would finally share what she knew. She eased forward on the couch to get the notepad.

"I'll get it, Jelly," said Lowell. He knew the notepad was still in the bathroom from where she'd first hidden from the detectives.

"Why don't we do this, Grace? We'll share with you what we've learned, the things we haven't told you yet, and you tell us what you remember. Maybe we can fill in the gaps for each other?" asked Detective O'Neal. Detective Grant nodded his agreement.

"We have more questions. Mostly surrounding the murder. We haven't charged your father with that because there's one piece that still puzzles us."

Lowell returned to the room, handed Grace her

notepad, and then headed to the kitchen for a slice of cold pizza.

"There's still food here, if anyone wants some," said Lowell. Grace was focused on the notebook. Both detectives politely declined.

"Okay," she said, flipping to the right page. "This is where I get confused." She looked up at both detectives and leapt into the deep end.

"WHEN I WAS LITTLE, I used to hide in my mother's closet. I'd crawl in the very back corner where it was dark, especially when I was scared. Sometimes it was just a comforting place to be, nestled amongst my mother's things. I remember my dad looking for me once, but he couldn't find me. My mother had an old mannequin on the floor in there and I'd wedge myself behind it. I didn't remember that until the other day when I saw one in a thrift shop. Anyway, her closet was my special hiding place."

"My mother made me recite a phone number, over and over. If I was ever in trouble or if something happened to her, she instructed me to dial this number. She told me what to say. She made me recite the number and practice what I should say. Except in my dreams, I'm in the closet holding the phone and I don't remember the number, let alone what to say. I'm holding the phone in my hand, but I can't remember what to do."

Detective O'Neal glanced at Detective Grant.

"What?" asked Grace. "That's something, isn't it?" She looked over at Lowell, who was now leaning against the doorway to the kitchen with a mouth full of cold pizza.

"Yes. It's something. We found a phone on the floor in the closet. Behind a mannequin, in fact. The phone was open and the dialled number showed, but a call had not been placed."

"What colour was the phone? I remember it being silver," said Grace.

"Silver? No, it was white. An old iPhone," said Detective Grant.

"Weird," said Grace. "I still don't remember the phone number." Detective O'Neal glanced at her notes.

"The phone showed 000. It was the number punched in, but not dialled," said Detective Grant, his voice clear. "The number for emergencies." Grace felt like she'd just been slapped.

"Are you familiar with 000, Grace?" Detective O'Neal asked.

"Yes, but dad said I should never call it because bad people listened in on those calls."

"Jesus," exhaled Detective Grant.

"I never knew why we were running. My father only told me some bad guys were after him. Later, when I got older and asked too many questions, he beat me."

"Why did you need to call 000 that night, Grace? Were you in danger? By your father or by other people?"

"My father. He came home, drunk or… well, now I know he was probably high. He kept repeating 'what did you do' to my mother. He was crazy. When she didn't answer, he hit her. She went flying across the kitchen. I couldn't move. I stood there clutching my Raggedy Ann doll, the one Nanny made for me. I remember my father screaming at my mother, but I don't remember what he said. Wait. I do remember something. She was his. That's what he said. Then he called her a whore. He liked to call me that, too. Later. More often recently." Grace took a breath and put her head in her hands. She sat like that for a few minutes, rocking back and forth. Memories of that awful night rushed into her head.

"Jelly," she heard Lowell's voice, but she shook her head. She had to get this out.

"He was on top of her with his hands were around her neck, choking her. Then, he was doing something with his belt." She shivered, dredging up the memory of her own attack. Dismissing it, she continued. She had to tell the detectives what she remembered.

"My mother… She looked straight at me, straight in the eye, and told me to go back to bed. But I just stood there and watched. She repeated it, begging me to leave. He didn't seem to hear anything, he was so focused on her. It was like I wasn't there. I was so scared. I finally ran back to the closet in their bedroom. I remember hugging my doll. She would protect me. Nanny pinky swore." Grace looked down at her ravaged fingers, picked at them absently. Whatever happened to dolly? Was it thrown out with the Dora backpack? When she looked up again, three faces looked intensely at her. She shook off the memory and continued.

"In the closet, I remember having a phone in my hand. But I couldn't remember the number. I heard dad grunting and breathing really hard. I know he was hurting her, but I still couldn't remember the number. Everything got quiet, so I crawled out toward the door. The silence terrified me. But I had to help her. I remember looking down the hallway and saw a red suitcase and my *Dora the Explorer* backpack, sitting by the front door. But then the screaming started again. It frightened me so much I ran back to the closet and picked up the phone again. I punched the number, but it wouldn't dial. The phone was cold now. Icy cold."

"So, you stayed in the closet after that, too scared to leave it. Is that right?" asked Detective Grant.

"Yes. I only remember sitting in the closet with the phone in my hands, unsure of the number Mummy told me to dial." Her voice was small, rising an octave, the voice of a little girl.

Detective Grant looked to Detective O'Neal and nodded to the file, holding out his hand. Something about the detective's demeanour had Lowell moving off the doorframe. Detective Grant held up a hand to stop Lowell from going to Grace.

"One piece of evidence that has been plaguing police, has to do with what killed your mother," he said.

"She wasn't strangled?" Grace asked. Detective Grant shook his head.

"No Grace. Your mother was shot." All the blood in her face drained away. The gun under her father's chest of drawers.

"My father had a gun in the apartment. In his bedroom," she said it so quickly she couldn't take the words back.

"We know. We found the gun. It matches the weapon used that night." Grace let out a cry that sounded like a strangled cat. She slumped over, her face back in her hands. Tears choked her.

"The thing is, the angle of the bullet doesn't make sense," Detective Grant continued, pulling a photo from the file. "The forensic scientists have told us that the shot came from a distance. So, we're wondering if someone else was there in the room. Did you hear or see anyone else besides your mum and dad?" He handed her the photo of the crime scene. She took it, her hands shaking, seeing the image from her nightmares in full colour.

"The markings on the picture show the gun had been fired from the hallway." Grant pointed at the arrows.

The hairs on her neck and arms prickled upright.

"No. I don't remember anyone else being there," Grace said weakly.

"Then there's the question of the angle. This is the part that's haunting us. The shooter would have been crouching. But we have another theory. Grace, is it possible it was a gun in your lap and not a phone?"

"What?!" Grace's head snapped up. "No." She felt sick.

"Look at this photo," he said, and handed her a second picture. It was the gun hidden under her father's chest of drawers. Her hands trembled like autumn leaves before a thunderstorm.

"Take your time and think back to that night. It was dark in the closet. You heard your mother screaming. You've told us she begged you to stay put no matter what, but you found her screams too hard to ignore. So, you went to your mother to see if you could help. You stood in the doorway and watched your father do unspeakable things to your mother. So, you ran into the bedroom and hid. Is that right?"

"Yes." Her voice barely a whisper, but her eyes remained transfixed on the gun. Until her own attack, she would never have thought her father would do such a horrible thing. He'd raped her mother. She knew that. Would he go so far to kill her too? It was possible. Seconds dragged into minutes.

"It wasn't a phone," Grace mumbled.

"Pardon?" asked Detective Grant.

"It wasn't a phone I was holding. I remember it being silver and it felt cold. It wasn't a phone. It was a gun."

She found Lowell's eyes and whispered, "I shot my mother."

Grace's thoughts were thick and heavy. Her head throbbed. She stared down at the photo of the gun. It all came back to her.

"When I scrambled back to the closet, I picked up the gun from my father's shoebox. He'd put it there... I don't know when. He told me to keep it a secret." Her mind was a muddle of images and suddenly she was that five-year-old girl. The one in her dreams.

"I couldn't tell Mummy. It was to protect us from the bad people, he told me. I remember picking it up with both hands. It was so heavy. When I went back to the kitchen, Mummy was on the floor with Daddy on top of her. His hands were around her throat, but she saw me. I know she saw me. She started shaking her head back and forth, but her eyes stayed on me. She kept telling me to go back. Or trying to tell me no. And she was crying. He was still... on her. The gun was so heavy, and my hands were shaking. I pointed the gun at Daddy. I needed him away from

Mummy, but he wasn't getting off her. Then…" She covered her ears, then dropped them quickly into her lap.

"The sound was loud, so loud. I fell back, on to my bottom. All I remember is blood. Everywhere. And Daddy, his head whipping around. He saw me but I couldn't move. He stood and pulled up his pants, really slowly, like it was slow motion. Then all of a sudden, he was right there in front of me, ripping the gun from my hands. He slapped me, really hard." As if in a dream, Grace raised her hand to her cheek, feeling the sting of the slap instead of her tears.

"He was then yanking me from the room. I looked back for Mummy, and all I saw was blood."

A few minutes later, she heard someone clear their throat. It was enough to bring her back to her reality. Wiping the snot that dribbled down into her mouth, Grace took a deep breath, looked at Detective Grant and asked for the answer she needed to know.

"Will you arrest me now? Will my father go free?"

Detective Grant studied her with the warm eyes of a grandfather.

"Is this all true, Grace?" he asked. His voice was quiet. Gentle. She looked at him, knowing she was about to throw away the freedom she so desperately wanted. Tears continued to stream down her cheeks. She sniffed, then nodded.

"It's true. I didn't remember before. We ran so I wouldn't be caught. We ran so the truth wouldn't come out." Shame engulfed her.

In that moment, she finally knew the truth behind her mother's death. But why didn't he just turn her in?

"Why would he not leave me in Melbourne?" she whispered. "That's what you wondered too, isn't it?"

"The only thing I can deduce, Grace, is to protect himself," said Detective Grant. "Your father was an extremely selfish man. You were a brilliant cover, especially if he could play the loving father. Abusive men can be like that. We knew he was violent toward your mother. I hesitated to have him as an informant for that reason, but… well, he had a suitable cover as a landscaper, and he spilled information like a leaky tap when he was high. I'm surprised he's not been caught before this. We were close to finding you, about ten years ago, and I'm sorry we didn't catch him then. We thought we had him, coming back to Melbourne on the Tasmania ferry, but the report came back it was a single man. No child."

"I was hiding in the van, under the seats," Grace said, looking at Lowell.

"Oh shit," the detective blurted impulsively. "I'm so sorry Grace. I truly am," said Detective Grant.

"It's okay. I should have told someone what he was like," she said, looking down at her now bloody fingers.

"From my experience," added Detective O'Neal, "I've seen a lot of children traumatised by their abusive parents, frightened at what would happen if they told someone. It happens more times than you would imagine that they just don't speak up."

"If you had told someone, I think your father would have had you both running before we even knew."

Bad things will happen if the truth comes out.

Her father's words rung in her ears.

Bad things will happen if the truth comes out.

Was this what Detective O'Neal was talking about? She was going to jail too. There was no question about that. She didn't have the 'organisation' after her, but jail would be an end to the life she dreamed of.

Grace stood slowly and walked to Lowell.

"I'm so sorry I got you caught up in this. But thank you for being my friend."

"Grace," Detective Grant said, coming over to stand behind her. She knew she was moments from being hauled out. So much for her freedom. Her new life. She looked into Lowell's eyes, saw her own deep pain reflected in them.

"Grace," the detective repeated. "We won't be charging you for your mother's death. You remember what happened. It will be hard for you to come to terms with that, and I'm sure it will take a while..."

Grace turned around quickly to face the detective, ignoring the dizziness.

"But...but I'm a murderer. I killed my mother," she wailed. Emotion overtook her. Her knees buckled. The detective caught her as she went down, and she sobbed into his chest.

"It's going to be okay," he cooed, trying to calm her.

"How?" Her voice was much louder and screechier than she meant for it to be. She pulled away from the detective quickly and looked at him in disbelief, feeling raw and vulnerable. He smiled at her.

What the...? She wiped the tears brusquely from her cheeks. Why the hell was he smiling? Was he sick? Was he just playing games with her? She'd confessed to killing her mother, and he was smiling? Was this a rouse? She snorted. Involuntarily.

"The law is on your side here, Grace. You were five, which is under the criminal age of responsibility. Besides, it was self-defence. Now, Michael will be locked away for a long time. He's still being charged with rape, attempted rape, violating an AVO, fraud, larceny, possession, dealing. All of that has nothing to do with your mother's death, but every one of those charges will stack up. We have a rock-solid pile of evidence against him. He wasn't a good man, Grace. Maybe he was good to you at times? But I'd say he cared more about protecting his own interests."

"Grace," the detective continued. "You've survived everything that's been thrown your way. You'll survive this too."

"The things my father said about my mother. That she was a drug user too, and a whore. Where they true?" The older detective looked surprised and shook his head quickly.

"No Grace. Probably furthest from the truth. I never met your mother, but I have learned a lot about her over the years. She was smart, independent, very beautiful, like yourself. She just fell in love with the wrong guy and got trapped. Like many women do. She couldn't find her way out, despite your grandmother trying desperately to help her. I'm sure your grandmother can fill in many of the blanks there, but the short answer is no. Your mother was a good person and she loved you fiercely. And, from all I've learned, she was trying to get you both out of the situation that night."

Lowell held his hand out to help her off the floor. Grace hesitated, but when he broke out into a huge goofy grin, she took his hand and let him wrap his arms around her.

"You're free, Jelly," he said. She didn't feel very free, though. The weight of this revelation felt like an elephant on her chest.

FIFTEEN MONTHS LATER

Grace stood at the arrivals gate at Tullamarine Airport in Melbourne, wearing a pale pink sundress and sandals, showing off her freshly painted bubble-gum pink toenails. Lowell's flight was late. She paced back and forth, scanning the arrivals board every few seconds. She only hoped he arrived before his mother, who was due to land half an hour later from Brisbane. She couldn't wait to share her news with him. She'd thought about telling him over the phone, but decided to wait. She wanted to see the look on his face.

She was still surprised to be standing in an airport. To her, airports represented freedom, something she was still getting used to. She'd never been in an airport until last year. It was too exposed, John told her over the years. No, not John. Michael. She was still getting used to that too, even with the trial over. God, she hated thinking about those months. Michael had fallen deep into his addiction. He was barely coherent during the trial. No, John was gone and whomever Michael was, he wasn't her father.

The arrival board flashed and Lowell's flight finally switched to 'landed'. Phew. She hadn't seen Lowell in six months, even though she talked with him every day. She leaned heavily on Lowell during the trial, and his mother too. But her rock was her grandmother.

Nanny. Grace smiled, thinking of this wonder woman in her life. Detective Grant kept his promise. He notified her grandmother the night Grace discovered her truth. Early the following morning, Nanny arrived at Lowell's front door, clutching Grace's Raggedy Ann doll. Grace flew into her arms, hugging her grandmother and the doll for a very long time, just as her world came crashing down around her.

Since then, Nanny became the centre point of Grace's recovery. She organised counselling sessions, made arrangements with the school, and accompanied Grace to the police station to finalise their statements. There wasn't a time that she left Grace's side. Neither had Lowell, for that matter. Together, they held her steadfast. Grace knew she'd be okay with them at her side.

Waiting for Lowell to come through the arrivals door, she thought about the day Nanny joined one of Lowell's yoga sessions. She'd joined Annie, Lowell's favourite client, in a 'boogie-off' dance competition once the yoga session was over. The pair came together like long-lost sisters. Her grandmother, easily a foot taller than Annie, her green eyes sparkling, laughed uproariously with the pink-haired firecracker. She'd looped Annie's purple feather boa around her hips, the feathers whirling as they swung back and forth to the music.

Her grandmother was a spitfire. She was as tall as Grace, and model thin. Her silver hair was cut short into a stylish pixie. Everything about her grandmother was edgy, yet somehow refined. Looking down at her own manicured nails, her cuticles now healed, Grace realised she'd never seen Nanny's bold red nails chipped, not once. Grace wondered if her mother would have been the same? Probably. With everything Nanny had shared with her, Grace was her mother's twin, right down to her obsession with writing. She'd discovered some of her mother's poetry. It was beautiful. Soft, flowing, descriptive. Grace was hoping to publish it someday. For now, she kept it for herself.

She was excited for this coming week. Lowell, his mother Nellie, and her Nanny would be celebrating Christmas and New Year's Eve together. Nanny had planned the entire week for them all. Grace only wished her mother was … no, she couldn't think like that. She couldn't think of what she'd done. Her psychiatrist told her she needed to focus on the present. Be grateful for what she had in her life. And she was. She thought about the relationship between her grandmother and Lowell. It was a mutual lovefest, although he admitted, right after meeting her, 'God help anyone who crossed her'. Grace had to agree.

At the trial, Nanny had gone for her father's jugular, keeping Grace firmly behind her. It would take a lot of therapy to get over the guilt of testifying against him, not to mention killing her mother. Her therapist constantly reminded her it was an accident. Maybe it was, but Grace knew the bullet simply missed its intended target.

After it was all over, Grace shed the last traces of her father by legally changing her name. She was Grace Baxter now, using her grandmother's maiden name, with no plans to change her name ever again.

The more she learned about Michael, the more she realised the truth: Michael was bad news. He had been, as Detective Grant predicted, only protecting himself. She still struggled with the kindness Michael had occasionally shown, but therapy taught her those times were rare and misleading. It was a calculated decision to take Grace, to get back at her grandmother. He truly hated the woman. In a cowardly act of spite and defiance, Grace learned during the trial that they'd squatted in a house around the corner from Nanny's. If Grace only knew then what she knew now. She still didn't understand why he was so hateful. Sometimes people snapped. She shook off the thought. She couldn't think about that either.

Finally, a flow of people emerged from the arrivals hall. She bounced from face to face, eagerly searching for Lowell. A minute later he strode through the gate, his smile broad. He was impeccably dressed as usual, wearing his much-loved jeans. He'd forgone the band t-shirts she'd gotten used to, and instead wore a long-sleeve, white linen shirt, the sleeves rolled up to his elbows. It was so good to see him.

"Jelly! Look at you. Looking fabulous!" He held out his arms.

"You too," she said, stepping into his embrace. They held each other for a moment, happy to be together again.

"Looks like Mum's flight is on time," Lowell said, glancing up at the arrivals board. "Let's grab a coffee while we wait. I'm sure you're eager for one."

They talked about the latest happenings at his yoga studio while they waited for their order. She asked him how Annie and the ladies were doing.

"Annie's on a roll. A few gentlemen have signed up for classes now. Annie's been hitting on them, so I'm not sure how long they'll last." She laughed, happy to know Annie was still living her best life. He asked about her grandmother, even though they would see her in less than an hour.

"Nanny is excited to see you guys. But God, you should see the decorations and the number of presents under the tree. Its obscene. But she's already shared the pictures with you already, hasn't she?" Lowell nodded. Of course she had. They were two peas in a pod. They picked up their order and found a table.

"So, I have news. I wanted to wait until I saw you," she said, excitedly. "I got a call from that publishing house I told you about. The one Miss O'Donnell put me in touch with. They said they were extremely impressed with my H.S.C. English assignment, and would like to expand it into a book." She paused a beat. "They offered me a book deal." She blushed. "Apparently, there are upsides to going viral while testifying against your father."

"Wow Jelly, that's great! Congrats!" He raised his cup in cheers. She bowed her head in acceptance of the praise.

"But there's more." She knew the book was a big deal,

but she'd gush about that later. "I've been working with a group who help find missing children. Nanny has been involved with them for years. They work with NAPCAN." Lowell looked confused at the acronym.

"It's the National Association for Prevention of Child Abuse and Neglect. The Salvation Army work with them. A bunch of places do."

"Great. And?"

"I'm going to work with some experts to write a series of articles for the Education department. It'll help kids know how to deal with abuse, what to do, how to cope, that kind of stuff. I can include things I wish I knew, strategies which may have helped me earlier. Plus, I'll be working with a global group who deal with child abductions."

"Whoa."

"I know, right? Which brings me to my other news. I'm changing my degree. I'm going into social services, with a focus on child therapy." His smile was infectious.

"That makes total sense. I can see you doing that, Jelly. Maybe you should get a double degree? You've got more discipline than anyone I know."

"Maybe, I just know I need to give back. The world since, you know, all that happened, has been nothing but kind to me. I'll probably be in therapy for the rest of my life, but I want to do something worthwhile out of what happened to me."

"I'm really proud of you, you know?" She felt the heat rise up to her cheeks.

"Oh, stop blushing. Gumption, remember? You have

tons of it." Nellie's flight arrival was announced over the airport speakers.

"Speaking of gumption. Let's go find my mother."

"I can't wait to see her. Plus, we're going to need all the help we can get to manage the ten bags you likely brought. How will we get them all home?" she teased. He rolled his eyes, confirming her suspicions. Lowell picked up his messenger bag while she tossed their coffee cups into the recycling bin.

"By the way, how many coffees is that for you today?" he asked, as they walked to the arrivals gate.

"Four. No, five." He hung his head in defeat. She would never give up coffee.

ACKNOWLEDGMENTS

This book began as a dream. Figuratively and literally. In 2016, I woke one morning thinking 'that would be a great scene in a book' and so, grabbing coffee (of course), I trundled downstairs to my 'office' to jot it down. Eighteen hours later, I was still writing. The story poured out of me like a raging river. I would have collapsed at my desk if not for my husband coming to the rescue with water, food and eventually, wine. Funnily enough, that scene never made it to the final version.

Without the insights in those early days from my Sydney writing group, Daniel would be an unrealistic white knight and Grace's character would be as savoury as eating cardboard. Thank you particularly to Lara, Jeanette, Avril and Ed, whose insights kept the book afloat and gave me more fodder to consider when turning the dream into a book.

Thank you to Jenny Breukelaar for her editorial

insights. As a result, chapters were scrapped, characters rewritten, and it was only then that I took a good, long look at what worked - and what didn't. I hope what is now published still made you gasp Jenny–in a good way.

My incredible Tasmanian Writer Friends: Nicole, Danielle, Phyll, Georgina, Kylie, Kat, Naomi and Matt. Thank you for the brainstorming and publishing insights. Most of all, thank you for your kindness and friendship.

To my 'Circle' - you know who you are. Thank you for always being there and cheering me on.

Thank you to Jimmy's Beach Caravan Park in Hawk's Nest, N.S.W. How could I not mention your kindness? Providing an extra night's stay gave me the time and space to finish the first draft of this book! I can't tell you how happy I was driving home, knowing I'd written my (first) novel!

To Philippa Jones: Thank you for helping me navigate Grace's potential legal mess. Your insight saved me a whole lot of creative manoeuvring around what may have been a disaster. Thank you also to my stepbrother, Jim Brock, for sharing his expertise regarding with my many Child Services questions. For both these areas, any mistakes are my own.

My Lovelies: Kim McDaniel, Shari Hamilton, Natalie Cooke, Bronwyn Clark, Angela Garwood, Trish Weiner, Nicole Alley and Agnes Jenkins. These are my *incredible* beta readers. Thank you for your insightful, honest, and encouraging feedback. I am humbled by your support and thoughtfulness. I truly could not do what I do without you.

To my readers of *Camino Wandering*: Your many kind words and positive comments have given me the incentive to keep writing. I can only hope you continue to enjoy my stories about 'women with gumption' (as I like to call them). And to the guy who left the early 1* review for *Camino Wandering*, commenting about his displeasure about swearing in a book… I hope you didn't read this one. But if you did, I look forward to seeing your next 1* review.

It's been twenty years since my mum died and I still think of her every day. I'm sure I drove her nuts with the constant tapping on my Corona typewriter many moons ago, but it was her fault! She gifted the typewriter to me when I was a 'tween, in an effort to encourage my creativity! (I guess it worked.) My mum was the person who taught me about resilience and love. When I write about women overcoming seemingly insurmountable challenges, my mum shines through each of these characters.

To my amazing daughter Natalie, who educates me daily (and I daresay she'd be surprised by that comment). She has become a great sounding board in my writing process. Natalie has always been an incredible young woman, but now she's an adult, she comes with her own pot of gumption. I feel incredible blessed she still wants to speak with me daily, no matter where we are in the world. Thanks for all you do and all you are, Nat. I'm massively proud of you.

Finally, to the guy who puts up with my schiz every day: my husband Richard. Thank you, my love, for sticking not only with me, but with Grace, Lowell, and all the other characters swirling in my head. I may not love hearing *all* your suggestions, but thanks to you, I'm a better writer and a better person. When I mentioned it was 'a package deal', way back when, I guess there was way more to it than we realised. ;-)

ABOUT THE AUTHOR

In 2011, Tara ditched the corporate desk, emptied her nest in 2017, and travelled the world for three years, working as a travel writer and photographer. Today, she lives in Tasmania, Australia. She has pivoted her writing focus to fictional stories, writing about women overcoming seemingly insurmountable challenges, revealing who they are and what they're made of.

If you enjoyed this book, you can find more of Tara's writing on her website, www.taramarlowauthor.com. Tara publishes a monthly newsletter, sharing information about the books she's currently working on, her writing process and other random nuggets.

Tara's novels are available via Amazon, Apple, Kobo, Barnes & Noble, and wherever you find your favourite books.

You can also find Tara on Facebook and Instagram.